A hen-pecked man discovers his voice is the most powerful instrument on Earth—and decides to make the most of it. . . .

A beautiful woman biologist finds out she has made an unfortunate sexual miscalculation on a planet inhabited by stallions. . . .

An unsuspecting rock-and-roll band goes on a gig that is—to put it mildly—out of this world. . . .

A space traveler heads for Mars—and receives a reception beyond all imagining. . . .

TIME-JUMP

**Ten unforgettable tales of
adventure in time and space**

TIME-JUMP

by John Brunner

A DELL BOOK

Published by
Dell Publishing Co., Inc.
1 Dag Hammarskjold Plaza
New York, New York 10017
Copyright © 1973 by John Brunner
Printed in the United States of America
First printing—December 1973

ACKNOWLEDGMENTS

INEXPENSIVE TIME MACHINES first appeared in *Galaxy*,
Copyright © 1965 by UPD Publishing Corp.

SPEECH IS SILVER first appeared in *Amazing Stories*, Copyright © 1965 by Ziff-Davis Publishing Co.

THE WARP AND THE WOOF WOOF first appeared in *Science Fantasy*, Copyright © 1966 by Science Fantasy.

THE PRODUCT OF THE MASSES first appeared in *Galaxy*,
Copyright © 1968 by UPD Publishing Corp.

AUTOMATIC TWIN-TUBE WISHING MACHINES first appeared in *Galaxy*, Copyright © 1966 by UPD Publishing Corp.

DEATH DO US PART first appeared in *Science Fantasy*, Copyright © 1955 by Nova Publications Ltd.

COINCIDENCE DAY first appeared in *Analog*, Copyright © 1965 by The Condé Nast Publications, Inc.

WHIRLIGIG first appeared in *Beyond Infinity*, Copyright © 1967 by John Brunner.

A SURVEY OF THE MEMBERSHIP first appeared in *Galaxy*,
Copyright © 1967 by UPD Publishing Corp.

NOBODY AXED YOU first appeared in *New Worlds*, Copyright © 1965 by New Worlds SF.

All stories have been specially revised by the author for this
publication.

CONTENTS

INTRODUCTION

One evening early in 1968 I was down at the BBC's television studios in Lime Grove, London, waiting to appear on a program named *Talkback* in which viewers who had complained about the content of TV broadcasts were invited to come and argue with authors, producers, directors or other people who were responsible for the item they disapproved of going on the air.

Apart from the presence of a lady who assured us that her local mental hospital was such a lovely place she wouldn't in the least mind being committed to it—a proposition which I felt was open to question—my part of the show went off without incident. During the first part, however, there was what you might call a warm exchange of views (*Anglice:* shouting match), and the disagreement centered on whether one should or should not milk a number of sacred cows to furnish material for a comedy series; such as royalty, religion, death—in general, matters which, if broached among a group of English-speaking adults, can be relied on to provoke an embarrassed hush followed by a loud and overhasty change of subject. (In your crowd it may be sex, communism or racial prejudice which causes this phenomenon. Same difference. The series concerned has brought those up as well.)

In the nick of time (because if someone else hadn't spoken up, I'd quite likely have made sure of never being invited back to the BBC by bursting in from behind the scenes), a man on the panel pointed out that at least since the days of Aristophanes, and perhaps for a good deal longer, comedy has drawn on the most awe-inspiring source material as a matter of course, because laughter is one of the instruments by which we exorcise our deepest fears. The ancient Greeks were accustomed to having their gods represented on the stage as drunks, lechers and incompetents—or that's how we'd judge them from a contemporary standpoint, anyway. That fact, it could be maintained, put them several generations ahead of us in terms of relative sophistication; I'm sure there'd be hell to pay if you depicted Jesus in a movie as being capable of losing his temper, even though there's clear Biblical evidence (the blasting of the barren fig tree, the driving of the moneychangers from the temple) to show that he actually did.

So what I'd like to ask you is this: How do you feel about the future?

Me, when I stop and think seriously about it, I get precisely the same gut-churning reaction as when I hear the engines of a jet airliner being revved up to maximum against the brakes before taking off across the Atlantic. It's half apprehension (because it's a matter of record that more planes crash during takeoff and landing than at any other stage of their journey) and half childish excitement. Somewhere in my belly the two collide head-on, and when we're safely aloft and the stewardess comes around to ask if I want a drink—yes, by golly, I do!

Likewise, I read in the paper or see on TV that some idiot has escalated a brushfire war or canceled a welfare program or done something else to ensure that he's going to be very cordially hated by a large number of people, and I think, "Well, it could mean that I'm going to be blown to bits tomorrow, or mugged in a dark alley by someone who disapproves of the color of my skin, or . . . !"

And it could. But, luckily, as a character in another book of mine once remarked, it isn't that we're *totally* stupid—we just display a tremendous aptitude for it. So far the miraculous gift of being able to realize when we're making fools of ourselves has saved us from succumbing to any irreversible manifestation of our silliness. We remain, however, victims of that ancient and subtle Chinese curse, "May you live in interesting times," and it's inevitably an uncomfortable sensation to find oneself under any sort of curse, subtle or not, the evidence for which is obvious and irrefutable.

Besides, whatever tomorrow may bring, we are certain it will be no less . . . interesting.

To laugh when you're frightened makes the shiver down the spine more bearable. That's why we invented sick jokes (not a recent innovation but one of the oldest forms of humor) and *comédies noires* and *grand guignol*. The specific cure for the dilemma in which you find that you think you ought to be sniveling with terror and yet somehow reason and instinct won't agree on that, is to mock. What is more (as French puts it with perfect insight), you mock yourself.

Of it.

It's because science-fiction writers, by the nature of their calling, take the future more seriously than most other people that there are so many black comedies and so few rib-tickling farces in the canon. It's for the same reason that, while I can guarantee that all the stories in this book are comedies, I decline to promise that all of them will split your sides.

The Germans have a term which English lacks, and it neatly spans the area where science fiction and comedy meet. They say *Galgenhumor:* gallows humor.

Right.

This is the humor of someone standing on the scaffold with the noose around his neck, distracting the executioner and the crowd with wisecracks in the hope that the cloud of dust on the horizon may—just by the slimmest of chances *may*—portend the arrival of a royal reprieve.

> The writ was at the Brig o'Banff
> Tae set Macpherson free,
> But they pit the clock a quarter afore
> An' hanged him frae the tree!

I know exactly how Macpherson must have felt. Don't you?

JKHB

GALACTIC CONSUMER REPORT NO. 1:

INEXPENSIVE TIME MACHINES

*(Extract from GOOD BUY, published
by the Consolidated Galactic Federation
of Consumers' Associations, issue dated
January 2329 ESY.)*

Introduction

Experiments with time travel on the Asimov-Notsodusti
principle were made on Logaia as long ago as 2107, but a
series of spectacular accidents, too notorious to be described in detail here, led to legislation confining its use
to rare and extremely costly government-authorized research trips.

About a century ago, however (recent feedback has
made the actual date so fluid as to be insusceptible of
definition) a posthumous discussion with Einstein enabled
Dr. Ajax Yak of the University of Spica to formulate the
fundamental equations of petrified-field theory. The light
shed on the subject by his celebrated postulate that yaktion
and re-yaktion are equally apposite so simplified time travel
that the legislation was subsequently repealed and a market
opened for the sale of time machines to the public. (An
operator's license is required on most planets, punch the
yellow keyboard of your computer for details.)

Acceptable standards for the safety and performance
of these machines have been laid down on Earth, Osiris,
Confucius, and a number of other worlds, and a Galactic
Standard is reportedly in draft. Unfortunately these do
not have the force of law except insofar as their exclusion
lists are concerned (see below). We think they should. As
our members will have noticed, cut-price time machines
are now being widely advertised and time travel is bidding
fair to rival space travel as a popular vacation pastime.
We cannot too strongly caution our members against
blind acceptance of the advertisers' claims.

Brands Tested

Most major home-appliance manufacturers offer time machines in their current catalogues, and we hope in due course to make a thorough survey of the field. However, those priced at ten thousand credits or less are most likely to sell in large numbers to inexperienced purchasers, so we decided to conduct tests on all the models we found available below that limit. As always, we purchased our samples anonymously through regular retail outlets.

We bought two samples of each of two models whose full list price was above our ceiling but which can be had for less through a discount agency (*Worldline Wanderer* and *Chronokinetor*); one each at regular and discount prices of two models whose list price is under Cr. 10,000 (*Super Shifter* and *Tempora Mutantur*); and two each of two models apparently sold exclusively in the discount market (*Anytime Hopper* and *Eternity Twister*—the latter, incidentally, being described as "imported").

In order to complete a full range of tests on all models, we bought replacements for samples that failed during the course of our survey except when it was clear that doing so would waste our time and your money.

Appearance and Finish

In general, all machines are of acceptable standard, although one of the diamond instrument lights in the *Worldline Wanderer* had a flaw, while the gold and platinum inlay used for the floor of the *Super Shifter* was rated "cheap and garish" by all but one of our test panel. The inside door handles of the *Anytime Hopper* came off the first time we used them and had to be replaced. A fifteen-centimeter length of size 9 waveguide tube fits the socket, and we recommend this be substituted prior to making any trips in the machine, as waveguide tube of this caliber is not easily available in many popular historical periods, and since—as a sensible safety precaution—the machine is invisible and intangible so long as the doors are shut, there can be no question of asking a helpful native to let you out. (Or anyone else, for that matter.)

The emergency kits of tools and spares are adequate on all but the *Eternity Twister,* whose ratiocinator proved to be broken; the service manual was printed back to front in classical Arabic (presumably a computer error at the factory), and the forty-seven spare transistors were found to be lumps of contaminated polystyrene.

Guarantees

None of the guarantees is wholly satisfactory. That for the *Worldline Wanderer* is almost acceptable, in that it guarantees replacement of any part developing a fault during the first hundred hours of subjective occupation, but the owner is obliged to make his own arrangements for the return of the faulty parts to the factory—not easy on a trip of any length.

We recommend taking out a policy for retemporation insurance; several companies offer these at reasonable rates.

The guarantee supplied with the *Eternity Twister* runs to forty-eight pages of small print and required a computer evaluation to make it comprehensible. It proved to render the purchaser liable to distraint of his entire property by the importers of the machine if he makes any claim against them for any reason whatever. We feel that this should *not* be signed and returned to the company as they request.

Power Source, Drive and Controls

The *Worldline Wanderer* has a built-in fusion plant, of high output and fair reliability, although the cork of the magnetic bottle kept coming loose on both our samples and was difficult to replace with the Möbius wrench supplied, as the handle is too short.

All the others, bar one, have conventional fission piles. Only the *Chronokinetor* offers automatic dumping of exhausted fuel rods; the others have to be cleared manually. The makers of the *Tempora Mutantur* operate an exchange service for their rods, a good idea, but as yet imperfect from the consumer's standpoint. One of our testers was instructed to dispatch a consignment of rods while visiting the standard target area of 1779 and had to wait until

1812 for the replacements owing to mislabeling of the package at the factory.

The exception mentioned above is the *Eternity Twister*, powered by NiFe batteries supplemented by a pedal-driven generator. The importers claim that this furnishes ideal exercise to toughen up users on the way to barbaric time zones. Our testers followed the directions supplied, but all except one (silver medalist for weight lifting in the last Jovian Olympics) found it necessary to rest up for a week or so on arrival. This would not perhaps be the ideal start to a family vacation.

In five of the six machines the drive mechanism is a recognizable variant of the original Yak design, and any qualified service mechanic ought to be able to cure minor faults. (N.B.: Mechanics are not available earlier than 2304 except to users of the *Super Shifter*, whose makers have launched a training scheme for native labor in a few popular vacation zones farther back. A list of these comes with the machine.)

We are unable to make a positive statement as to the drive mechanism of the *Eternity Twister*, as the petrified field is generated in a black box labeled "Not To Be Opened." Attempts to inspect the interior resulted in messy, though not fatal, explosions. We consider this a serious design fault.

The controls on the cheaper machines, though stark, are adequate, with fair accessibility. We faulted the *Chronokinetor* because its three-vee display is reflected by the master time-range dial and makes the pointer difficult to read; the *Tempora Mutantur* because the dashboard is devoted to three-vee, piped music, sensishow outputs and perfumolator orifices, while the controls are on the arms of the operator's chair and can easily be activated by a careless elbow; and the *Worldline Wanderer* because the forward- and reverse-lever had been mislabeled on one of our samples: the first trial filled the testing lab with a horde of noisy and ill-dressed savages, later identified as Mongols, who defied our best efforts to return them to the machine and eventually had to be deported under a government regulation forbidding unauthorized entry to the present.

The *Eternity Twister* has a good range of controls and

instruments. Inspection revealed, however, that four out of a total of eighteen of them are not connected to anything. One of the range-finding dials on the *Anytime Hopper* has to be read in a mirror, but its pointer has not been made to rotate counterclockwise to compensate. The makers claim that it can be read directly, but if this was the intention, we think they should have included with their standard equipment a jar of liniment suitable for stiff necks.

Performance

As already mentioned, the Galactic Standard has not yet been published. We took the Confucian Standard CS as the basis for our tests, modifying it to the more stringent requirements of the Terrestrial Standard TS in respect of excluded zones.

First we measured the radius of the petrified field (CS and TS: five meters). All passed except two.

On one sample of the *Anytime Hopper* the field collapsed to half size during a test jump to 1898, leaving the tester's head in that year and his feet in the present. Repairs were speedily put in hand, but unfortunately an enterprising carnival operator discovered the tester's isolated upper portion and for some eight hours before rescue was effected employed it as a novel target in his sideshow. (This was of the type known as an "Aunt Sally," in which contestants received prizes for their accuracy in hurling wooden balls.)

The importers of the *Eternity Twister* state in their advertisements that the radius of their machine's field is "in accordance with the relevant Standards." One of our samples managed 4.1 meters, but the other never did better than 3.7. The *Worldline Wanderer* and the *Super Shifter* expanded to 10 meters without difficulty, and we are lobbying for this to be made the minimum for the Galactic Standard.

Next we carried out tests to determine range and accuracy. The CS lays down 5,000 Confucian years (about 4,762 Earthside Standard Years) as the shortest qualifying range, with an accuracy of plus or minus one month over ten repetitions at any lesser distance.

All sustained this over ranges below about 1,000 ESY. However, none was satisfactory on longer trips. In particular, one sample of the *Chronokinetor* landed twice in the Upper Pleistocene and the other in the Triassic owing to power surges. Both performed satisfactorily after we replaced the pile-moderators. The *Worldline Wanderer* has a repeatable extreme of 11,421 ESY, well in excess of the Standard, but at this high power level the cork kept coming out of the bottle.

The *Eternity Twister* records one maximum of 2,389 years, but this was not repeatable on either sample, and the average for both was one year seventeen days. One sample refused to go anywhere until the fuses had been replaced with five-centimeter busbars, while on the other the insulation burned out. Inspection revealed that it consists of badly tanned animal hide. We substituted a modern synthetic, but it proved impossible to get rid of the smell.

Finally we turned to the question of excluded time zones, and here applied the TS rather than the CS because the TS stipulates a greater conformity with people's prejudices.

Some confusion exists as to the reason for having exclusions, so a word of explanation may be in order. It is often thought that excluded zones are those highly susceptible to paradox feedback, in which casual tourists might upset the sequence of cause and effect. It is true that such zones are excluded, but not by us. They are patrolled by armed Temporal Police generally believed to be based around 10,600 ESY, and there is no question of tourists being able to get at them.

What we are now referring to are the zones surrounding events in the traditional version of which certain pressure groups have a vested interest: for example, the wanderings of the Children of Israel, the meditation of Buddha under the bo tree, the Sanctification of Emily Dong, the Aspiration of Bert Tuddle, and so forth.

On virtually all planets the only legislation governing the use of time machines (apart from operator's licence regulations) concerns the automatic cutouts with which any machine offered for sale on that world must be fitted. To some extent, these can be varied at the wish of the purchaser, so that on Earth one can choose from at least a dozen rival Christian lists, but the chance of obtaining a Koranic list on New Jerusalem is effectively nil (and the attempt is punishable with a heavy fine). And so forth.

No machine can be held to have passed the Standard unless it operates according to at least one of these lists, of which there are some two hundred. To secure as large a share of the market as possible, manufacturers generally offer a basic range of about twenty, with others optional at additional cost.

It would have been a prohibitively long job to try all the lists on all the machines, so we chose ten of the most popular, ten in average demand, and ten favored by minority groups. Our report follows:

Worldline Wanderer: Excellent for all Euro-American lists, including Judaic and Catholic, but poor on Asiatic and only fair on the remainder.

Super Shifter: Good in all areas except Moslem (the Hegira cutout failed on both samples).

Tempora Mutantur: Good, but unlikely to be favored by Neo-Pagans, as the list of available extras does not include the period of Julian the Apostate.

Chronokinetor: Excellent for Hellenic Revivalists (it is made by a Greek firm), fair in other areas.

Anytime Hopper: Fair to good in all areas except that the Wesleyan list is faulty; it proved possible to witness the composition of at least seven hymns.

Eternity Twister: Not rated. There are cutouts, and on the surviving sample of the two tested they operate well, all things considered. However, their operation is either absolutely arbitrary or geared to some exclusion list not available to the testing staff. Our testers meticulously visited every area supposed to be inaccessible. An indication of the seriousness of the fault: the unfortunate tester assigned to check on the zone of the Aspiration of Bert Tuddle returned to the present suffering from uncontrollable hysteria, and his report was delayed for three hours while we tried to make him stop laughing.

Value for Credits

Apart from the episode of the invading Mongols, the *Worldline Wanderer* performs well and meets the various standards we applied to it. We therefore name it our Best Buy. Those prepared to sacrifice performance to greater comfort may prefer the *Super Shifter*, which is less expensive, and those who bore very easily indeed may like the *Tempora Mutantur's* wide range of entertainment facilities. We do not, though, feel that any of these machines should be bought without a good retemporation policy.

And we do NOT under any circumstances recommend the purchase of an *Eternity Twister*. After the episode of the burning insulation, we sent samples of the animal hide to be analyzed. When it turned out to be Logaian lizard skin, we became suspicious and carried out further inquiries.

It turns out that these machines are being imported from 2107. They were built to the design of a self-taught "scientist" named Brong, who was left with about thirty million of them on his hands when time travel was restricted by law. Taking advantage of the recent repeal of these regulations, the importers now marketing them bought his entire surplus at a price alleged to be Cr. 18 apiece for resale at Cr. 3,500. We have reported this blatant profiteering to the Galactic Chamber of Commerce. Our advice is that even the purchase price of eighteen credits is too high. We disposed of ours to a scrap dealer: the best we could get was Cr. 11.

SPEECH IS SILVER

None of the company guards attempted to stop Jeremy Hankin as he walked toward the gleaming facade of the building across which was inscribed in huge letters the name of the Soundsleep Corporation. They recognized him, even without the makeup he was compelled to wear for the publicity pictures the company used, and knew that he could come here whenever he liked: a privilege granted by the doubtless very grateful directors. After all, they owed him a great deal.

Since his wife had left him, he had been coming here more and more often, seldom speaking to anyone—for the last several times not talking at all—but merely wandering with a wistful expression from floor to floor, peering curiously through the glass doors of the offices, acknowledging the greetings of impressed junior staff, hearty executives, and diffident clients with a uniform forced smile and a staccato nod.

Occasionally a bitter look came and went on his round, pale face, but it never lasted long enough for anyone to note its passage and start wondering.

The building covered an entire block, with three entrances. Over the past month he had formed the habit of leaving by a different door from that by which he had entered. The company guards would not expect to see him again once he had vanished inside.

The top four floors were Soundsleep's, the remainder rented. Very occasionally he had gotten out of the elevator at a lower level and stood looking at the names of other companies painted on the opaque doors there. He had never summoned the courage to investigate further, though, and for him the building existed as a kind of three-dimensional chessboard perched on top of a column of vaguely luminous mist. In and out of this mist, impinging on his awareness when they shared an elevator with him or brushed past him in the lobby, were the other occupants of the building. He would look at them and try to guess which of them were customers of Soundsleep; in particular, he would look at the young girl secretaries and wonder how many of them he spoke to every night—for how many of them he might be a publicly acknowledged bedfellow.

He took his usual up elevator, the first, and without apologizing for reaching past another passenger, pushed the button for the next-to-uppermost floor. The very top was where Soundsleep kept its most valuable commodity, and there was no direct service. Staff and visitors alike had to get out on one of the three other floors the company used, where there was little to mark it off from any other business corporation: small offices and large, more or less expensively furnished according to the status of the occupants, glass-partitioned or walled-in, allotted phones of black or colored plastic, prints or original paintings, in accordance with a subtle pecking order. But few companies could have matched the graphs displayed on every floor charting the growth of the venture from nothing, past the discontinuity of the Great Search, and thereafter up, and up, and *up*. . . .

It was Mary who got him involved, who stopped when he would have hurried by the street-corner booth and the urbane young man with the recorder, whose eyes brightened as she recognized reality behind what might have been a mere publicity stunt. Then the name on the portable booth meant little; one could tell from the puzzled faces of the crowd around that the reason for the young man's repeated challenge was known to very few people as yet.

A trifle dismayed at Mary's interest, yet gallantly falling in with her wishes—for he was very proud of his young and pretty wife, and their marriage was two years new—he stopped, as she had done, and took her hand.

"What's all this about?" he murmured, scanning the gaudy sides of the booth for some explanatory poster and finding only cryptic advertising teasers.

"It's the Great Search," Mary answered. "It was mentioned on TV last night. It's the Soundsleep company."

Soundsleep? He turned the name over in his mind and finally gave her a blank, inquiring smile.

"Oh, you must have heard of them!" Briefly an expression of annoyance turned down the corners of her red, ripe mouth, and he felt the inevitable heart-stopping pang of alarm that accompanied any falling short in his ability to live up to the image she had made of him. "They've only been servicing very rich people up till now, but they've got some new technique and they're going to make it available to everybody for practically nothing!"

He groped in memory. Associations still eluded him. He ventured at last, eyes still on the urbane young man who challenged passerby after passerby with his portable recorder, "Something to do with curing insomnia?"

"Oh, Jerry!" She sighed; he might have hoped that, if his mistake was especially ludicrous, she would chuckle, but Mary was Mary. "It's this thing where it tells you in your sleep how to straighten out things that went wrong during the day!"

Click! Some ill-tempered objections raised in a technical journal he had leafed through, by the vice-president of a firm making psychotherapeutic chemicals—something about automatic analysis. "Got it," he said aloud. "So what's the Great Search they're organizing?"

"They're looking for people with the right voices," Mary told him patiently. "A man and a woman who'll do all the recording. So then you just connect this gadget to your phone when you lie down for the night, and then it tells you to go to sleep so you won't lie awake worrying about things that went wrong earlier, and then it tells you—"

He didn't mean to interrupt; he never cared or dared to be rude to this marvelous girl who had married him for some reason he couldn't fathom. But he said then, "Yes, yes! I get the picture. Shall we move on?"

It was probably the slight nervousness always induced by being in the center of a crowd that set him on edge, he realized—that, and the curious, hungry intentness with which all eyes devoured the current subject of the urbane young man's attentions. He hated to be conspicuous, placed in the spotlight, and he knew Mary wished he were pushy and could stand out more from the mass, so she might quite well insist on his making a recording here.

Whatever they were required to say, the men addressing the microphone weren't spending more than a minute each on it, and the urbane young man was already eyeing the Hankins with a thoughtful expression.

"You're going to enter," Mary said with determination. "You've got a lovely voice. I've always told you that. In fact, I think it was maybe more for your voice than anything else that I married you. Especially in the dark. When you talk to me after putting the light out, it makes me—"

"Mary, *honestly!*" he whispered, feeling a hot, red current in his cheeks and glancing around with a frantic prayer that no one had overheard.

She giggled. "Well, it's true, isn't it? Which ought to make you a very good candidate for this job of talking to thousands of women in their bedrooms."

"Oh, please *stop it!*" He felt his blushes grow fiercer yet. Somehow he had never adapted to the standpoint Mary insisted was the normal one: believing that something which everyone did need not be treated as completely private. Once in a while he wondered whether she talked about it with her women friends, but he hated even wondering, and always shifted his mental gears with rigid self-control. "Anyway, it's probably just a publicity gimmick—they more than likely have the person lined up for the job already, and when they unveil him, it'll turn out to be the chairman's son."

"You're trying to crawl away, aren't you?" Mary murmured. "Well, I'm not going to let you. I'm very proud of that nice voice of yours, and I think you ought to go in for the competition."

"But—"

"Good gracious, Jerry! Anyone would think it cost money to enter and you were down to your last pennies! You don't even have to say very much—I saw it on TV, how they can take just two or three words and analyze the recording to see if this is a suitable voice or not."

And then the urbane young man was approaching, sharp-eyed, dark-clothed, holding his microphone like a gun pointed at the victim Mary had trapped for him.

"This is my husband," she announced firmly. "I think he ought to go in for your competition."

"Anyone and everyone is welcome to enter," the urbane young man purred. Hankin drew himself together with a terrible effort; the damage was done now, the stare of the crowd was focused on him, and he could not compound the suffering by behaving like an idiot. He must at least do Mary credit in this predicament.

Swallowing hard, he croaked at the urbane young man. "Uh—what do I have to say?"

"Anything you like, sir. To recite your name and address would probably suffice, though if you care to provide us with a longer sample for analysis we'd be obliged."

He took the shortest road to salvaton and identified and located himself. Then he pushed aside the microphone, took Mary's hand, and hurried away down the street.

Shivering, he came abruptly back to awareness of the present. He was staring up at the upward leap of the Soundsleep Corporation's fortunes that followed the date of the Great Search on the grid of the boastful graph. Nervous, he turned to see if anyone was watching him. There was someone: a pert, silvery-blond girl carrying a thick file of papers. She smiled as he looked her over.

"You're Mr. Hankin, aren't you? We've never actually met but, of course, I've seen you around the offices. You must be terribly proud when you look at the chart and see what a difference your voice made to Soundsleep!"

She paused as if expecting him to say something in that famous voice, but he didn't speak. Disappointed, she went on, "Well, I just wanted to tell you I think you're wonderful! I take the Soundsleep service myself—of course, I get it at discount because I work here—and I'm sure it's the voice that counts really, not the things you say, because they're quite ordinary and any fairly sensible person could work them out. What makes the difference is the voice. It's kind of—well—*persuasive,* isn't it?"

He shrugged and nodded and smiled and turned back to his contemplation of the graph, hoping that when he looked again she would be gone.

She was. He strode rapidly along the carpeted corridor until he reached a men's room. He listened for several

seconds, trying to determine whether it was empty; when
he convinced himself it was, he slipped inside.

He went to the farthest of the toilet booths, bolted the
door, and sat down on the lid of the toilet to wait.

When the letter from Soundsleep came, stating that he
had been selected out of three-quarters of a million candidates to provide the voice in which they would record the
tapes for their new mass-consumption service, he was
appalled. By now it was known that the Great Search
itself had doubled the company's client list, simply by
publicizing its existence, and plans were afoot to launch
the full-scale service with an hour-long TV spectacular and
exposure of the successful candidates to an audience esti-
mated at fifteen million.

"Do you mean you're not going to do it?" Mary demanded.

"Of course not!" he snapped. "Me go in front of all
those people? Reporters banging on the door all day and
night? Hysterical women planted by the publicity agents
to swoon when I appear? Life would be unlivable—I
couldn't call my soul my own!"

There was a long silence. Eventually Mary said, "I
don't think you have any guts."

He blinked at her vacantly.

"No guts," she said again. "I decided to marry you because I thought you did have—some sort of drive, some
sense of wanting to get ahead. I've watched you for two
long years now, night and day. Daytime, you're satisfied
to let things roll as they go—you don't take opportunities
when they present themselves, you don't go looking for
them when they don't. No guts. And what's true in the
daytime is true at night as well."

He looked at her face as though they were strangers,
and read there something yet more appalling than the
contents of the letter in his lax hand.

"But—but after people have been married for some
time, this kind of thing is bound to . . ." He abandoned
the hollow words, for she was shaking her head with
emphasis.

"Not 'bound to'," she declared. "I've checked up with

some of my girlfriends. Kitty's been married almost eight years, and she says Horace is like a teenager."

"You mean you actually discussed matters like that with a woman like Kitty?" He was shaking so much he had to join his hands.

"Oh, darling!" At once she was all melting, coming to hug him around the waist and look up at him with wide, imploring eyes. "I only wanted to find out if I was failing you in any way—if there was something I could do to *encourage* you. I'm sorry I made that dreadful crack about not having any guts, but I'd have thought—I really would have thought—that when a chance like this came along you'd jump at it."

So finally, afraid to lose her, he gave in.

In those far-off days of five years ago, Soundsleep operated from two floors of an old building in a somewhat rundown area, but even then there was the vigorous sense of a go-ahead organization transforming the dusty, shabby setting. Three men talking obsessively among themselves greeted him and brought him into a conference room where three others were already assembled. They put him into a chair at the bottom end of a long table and themselves sat down, ceasing to talk as though a switch had been pulled.

"This is Jeremy Hankin, the contest winner," said the oldest of the men who had escorted him in.

Silence occupied the next thirty-odd seconds. Then a red-haired man of about thirty, who had been in the room when Hankin arrived spoke up.

"That face won't photograph very well. Too round and smooth. Have to add some contours. Restyling the hair will help a bit, I guess, but—"

"This profile isn't bad," interrupted a balding man on Hankin's other side. "It's the weight that worries me. Have to trim that waistline a good four inches. They look for a lean type—traditional authoritarian ectomorph."

"I don't agree with the survey you're referring to," the redhead said. "Whichever way it goes, though, it's liable to be tough. Welland, couldn't you have got us better material to work with?" He glanced at the man who had introduced Hankin.

"How is it Welland's fault?" the balding man objected. "A voice and a face don't necessarily tie up. And with the woman we've scored damned near a hundred percent."

"The hell!" said the redhead morosely.

"Like it or not, she just can't be a busty twenty-year-old!" the balding man snapped. "Men won't take advice from an image like that. Got to be a woman of mature years, experienced, tolerant, not holding out the threat of permanent emotional ties, fine for a weekend in bed and a pipeline for inside data about the wiles of the opposite sex—"

Boiling up inside Hankin to this point had been a fearful sense of inanimate existence, as though for these people he didn't count as a man, only as merchandise. Now he found his tongue and croaked at them.

"What *is* all this? I thought it was my voice which concerned you, not my appearance!"

"Hm?" The redhead gave him a startled glance. "Oh, your voice? We have that already. We—"

"Just a second, Ted." Welland cut in with quiet authority. "I guess I should apologize for my colleagues' manners, Mr. Hankin. But you'll forgive them, I hope, when I show you just what it is they've been doing for the past eight solid years. Not to put too fine a point on it, you're the package rather than the goods."

"I—I don't understand," Hankin said feebly. Every now and then in his life he had come up against someone who made him feel totally inadequate, and here were six of them to cope with at once. Welland in particular breathed assurance, and Hankin was already sure that no matter what happened he would never be able to stand up and tell him to go to hell.

"I'll try and make it plainer, then," Welland promised with patronizing calmness. "You're familiar with our methods, aren't you?"

"I guess so," Hankin muttered. "You start by hypnotizing your clients, leaving a post-hypnotic suggestion which sends them to sleep under standard conditions: bed, darkness and the signal from the phone attachment, which you supply. They then report on anything that went wrong during the previous day, anything that embarrassed them or upset them and might cause insomnia or brooding and depression. Uh . . . then the hypnotic trance makes them accept the advice that is offered to straighten things out."

"You understand it very well." Welland smiled. "But I sense that something still puzzles you."

"Well, yes. I don't see how you can provide so much individual attention on an automatic service. Already you claim customers in the tens of thousands—you can't offer individual therapy to that many people!"

"It isn't therapy, except in the most general sense," Welland said. "What we're selling, in fact, is confidence. Assurance. Comfort. And—oh, we don't make any secret of it! —the way we do this is the same as astrologers and others such have been using for centuries: carefully planned ambiguity. We choose for each client a standard program that she—or he, but eight out of ten of them are women—will continue to receive regardless of what's actually been happening. We have sixty-odd standard programs now, and we're expanding. The content of the program can be rationalized by the sleep-waking mind of the hearer and the following day the impression is left that excellent advice has been given. But it's the subconscious mind, not the exterior influence, that leads to the solution of personal difficulties."

Hankin swallowed to ease the dryness in his throat. He said, "But if you have a genuine neurotic, then—"

"Oh, we insist on being told whether a new client is undergoing analysis or any other psychiatric treatment. We then request the therapist's permission before enrolling her—I keep saying 'her,' but I've explained why. Usually it's given with enthusiasm, because we do offer a unique service. You see, if the therapist wishes, we can arrange to have his specific instructions relayed to the client in place of any or all of the standard programs selected for her."

Somehow Welland exuded the impression that everything had now been explained; anyone who had more questions must be of inferior intelligence. Embarrassed beyond description, Hankin said doggedly, "But if you're already in this position, I don't see why you had to go through all this charade of finding someone with a particular voice, especially since"—he glared at the redhead—"you say you have it already! I guess this must mean that the recording I was fool enough to make during your Great Search would be enough even if I was struck dumb this instant."

"Hmmm!" Welland put the tips of his fingers together and leaned back in his chair. "It'll take a few minutes to elucidate that, I'm afraid. What happened was this. We began to discover, quite early in the history of Sound-sleep's service to the public, that certain apparently excellent programs were getting nil results. We traced this fault not to the substance but to the presentation of the material. We'd been using anyone who came handy to make up the tapes—chiefly unemployed actors and actresses with good speech training. Some of the voices we'd picked on turned out to provoke subliminal hostility reactions in the clients, with consequent resistance to the words spoken. So we called together a team under Ted here—Ted Mannion—and set them to work to find an optimum voice. And they did it. It's a beauty! In fact, our latest standard program uses it already."

"A—an *artificial* voice?" Hankin forced out.

"Surely, why not? We've had crude voders for almost half a century. Soundsleep just had a greater incentive to perfect the device than other researchers in the field. By the way, when I say 'an' optimum voice, we have one for men, too—a woman's voice, of course—but in that case we may have to reconsider our first choice."

"It's the gay boys and the dykes that really throw us," the redhead muttered with a scowl.

"Shut up, Ted," Welland ordered with unruffled good humor. "I guess by now you want to know where you come in, Mr. Hankin. Well, that's quite simple. We needed a far wider base of client support—that's fancy jargon for a lot more money—in order to pay for having all our standard programs remade using the artificial voice. It's expensive. So I dreamed up the idea of a nationwide search for the man and woman with the optimum natural voice. You happened to have it. When we analyzed your brief recording, despite the evident nervousness, we found an incredibly close match to the artificial optimum. Indeed, if you'd been a trained actor, or someone used to public speaking, we'd even have considered using your voice in fact as well as—ah—for official purposes."

"But you're not going to," Hankin muttered. Ever since he had yielded to Mary's plea and agreed to make this appointment, he had been steeling himself for the ordeal with the reassuring belief that he genuinely was going to be indispensable—that he was going to be the instrument whereby a great many insecure, anxious people were helped. Now, in the twinkling of an eye, that prop was removed from him.

Unconscious of the bomb he had planted under Hankin's precarious self-confidence, Welland gave a bright nod.

"That's right! All we ask of you is the sole right to use your name and identity in association with our optimum male voice. The actual demands made on you will be few —public and television appearances, where we'll keep your involvement to a reasonable minimum, photo sessions and so forth for publicity purposes." He waved an airy hand. "And for this we'll pay twenty-five thousand a year for a guaranteed five years with excellent prospects of renewal. What do you say?"

Hankin said nothing. That was the first shadow of what came after.

It was during rehearsals for the TV spectacular to put his name and face before the public that Mary met Welland for the first time. He noticed them talking together and kept trying to see what had become of them from then on, but the irritable program director finally had to shout at him, and thereafter he concentrated on getting the business over with.

He hated it, every second of every minute of every hour. It wasn't even the money that kept him at it. It was knowledge of how much store Mary set by the money.

And thinking of Mary, and what he could suddenly no longer do for her, made him more depressed than ever before in his life.

Perhaps it was as simple as it appeared; perhaps he had known that it was indeed his voice—mellow, quiet, rich-toned, musically inflected—which had attracted her to him, and his belief in this had sustained his physical capacity to satisfy her younger desires. Abruptly, his voice was no longer his; it was something concocted artificially by a group of computers, scaled to a grand average reaction pattern mapped over a huge section of the population.

He wished all this could end, and his life could jell again into the unexciting but bearable form it had had until now.

But it didn't.

The TV spectacular was a tremendous success. After it there was a party which he had hoped to escape, for they had had to fill him with tranquilizers and he was not allowed to drink. All he wanted to do was sleep. But for Mary's sake he endured it until past midnight, seeing that she was enjoying the attention so many half-tipsy men were giving her. And she was looking marvelous, that was certain. She had gone shopping with the first advance against his fee and come back with some exquisite gowns and a superb new hairstyle.

At twelve-thirty he realized she wasn't there any longer, and neither was Welland.

After the divorce—which wasn't followed by remarriage on either side, for Welland grew bored and glossed it all over with a payment out of Soundsleep's by then astonishing profits—Hankin fell almost completely silent and into near total apathy. He had more money than he knew what to do with, but if he went anywhere in public, so thorough had the publicity about him been, that he could not have a moment to himself. Columnists came to pump him for gossip, women came to confess that they heard his voice every night (and usually also to try to tell him of their intimate problems, not being completely satisfied with reciting them to the impersonal attachment which shared their pillows), and on two occasions frustrated husbands tried to pick fights with him under the impression that he had seduced away the affections of their wives.

He dropped out of sight for over a year. Not until the time came when they took over this city block and built on it the new Soundsleep Corporation Building did he venture to return to the environment that had wounded him so deeply. It was chiefly wistful curiosity that drew him. He was wondering what use Welland and his colleagues were making of the golden shower he had brought down on their heads.

On that first visit to the new premises, he was lucky enough not to encounter Welland—he was off with some recent conquest, taking a vacation in the Bahamas. Ted Mannion, however, had conceived a kind of pity for him bordering on affection and, with an odd mixture of gruffness and tenderness, revealed to him the secrets of the web Soundsleep now spun across the entire continent.

Hankin watched in silence as the gleaming silvery machines were displayed in turn: those that analyzed the reports on new clients and decided which of the now well over a hundred standard programs best suited their condition; those that actually sent out the prepackaged reassurances; those that could amend the standard programs to accord with special requests from psychiatrists who might have the clients in their care—simple, these last, for one only needed now to deliver the words into a recorder microphone and the computers revised the sound of the voice automatically.

"It's amazing what that voice of yours has done for us," Mannion said.

"Yours," Hankin contradicted. That had become the typical length of his utterances: a single word, preferably a monosyllable. The voice had been his, and now no longer was; he felt obscurely that it was wrong for him to use it.

Mannion shook his head. "No, without the reality of yourself to attach it to—without your pictures, your name, your TV appearances—it would just have been a good, serviceable, general-purpose voice. Having you to hang it on, people regard it as the voice of a friend. Do you realize you have two hundred and seventy thousand women friends?"

Hankin turned away with an empty shrug. On the walls were pictures of the image-Hankin built up by the corporation; playing on looped-tape TV recorders in the lobby were cuts of the image-Hankin from the Soundsleep-sponsored shows on which they had compelled him to appear.

That's not me. "We'll have to add some contours."

Mannion hesitated. He said at last, "Sorry, Hankin. For

the moment I'd clean forgotten about your wife. If it's any consolation, I think Welland's a bastard, too. But he's got the drive. Without him, we'd be what we started out as: an exclusive service for a few rich folks. I like it better handling clients by the scores of thousands."

As usual, Hankin did not reply. And finally, when the silence had stretched elastically, Mannion said, "You make me feel like a thief, standing there and not opening your mouth. Exactly as though I'd stolen your voice. Goddammit! But I wasn't to know it was *yours!*"

The words went arrow-straight to the heart of Hankin's suffering, and he found himself very briefly able to speak, packing into the few seconds of release a whole disastrous world of meaning.

"I don't know why you had to have me, Mannion! You should have hired an actor, trained him to behave the way you wanted, grafted on the artificial voice!"

Which was, of course, what they had decided to do. Though the five years were not yet up, there was another Jeremy Hankin in training: a younger man, slightly thinner, whose face was close enough to the image-Hankin to be made over with a little trouble, and whose voice would never be his own but an elaborate facsimile of the Hankin voice generated in a miniature voder concealed under his left armpit.

There had been a great deal of progress since the Great Search.

It was when he learned this that Hankin began to come back and to walk around the four floors at the top of the Soundsleep building, to pry and listen and hope against hope for some means of reconnecting to reality. Everything seemed to have been drained out of his life by Soundsleep: his wife, his future plans for a family, his job —because it was neither possible nor necessary to continue working when he was a pensioner of the corporation. And now they wanted to filch his very identity, reassign it to another man, a stranger who was not plagued by the loss of his voice because it wasn't his. It must be somewhere here; it must all be concealed in these four floors, most likely on the topmost, where the shining machines every night spun a web of Hankin-words into the minds of thousands upon thousands of borderline-neurotic women. Pretty or ugly, single or married, the voice swayed their lives. Gave purpose to them.

So, logically, the lost purpose of his own life must be here, being diluted and distributed to all those clients who nightly waited for his marvelous voice.

Five years running out, like sand in an hourglass. They won't have told the company guards, they won't have told the pretty little silvery-blond typist who gets the service at a discount because she works here. . . . but Welland told me.

They proposed to invoke a clause in the original contract which forbade him to let or assign use of the identity "Jeremy Hankin" and its voice to anyone but the Soundsleep Corporation. And that included himself, the former owner. Five years had passed, and they wanted someone not plagued by weaknesses and faults. They wanted someone who could be exploited to the full without worrying whether his tongue was tied tonight. From tomorrow they would pay him not for being Jeremy Hankin, but for being someone else. Anyone else. Pick a name and change to it for the rest of his life; pick a face and have it put on over the original.

Welland, goddam you to hell. You stole my wife, you stole my voice, and now you're stealing me. . . .

The time was seven o'clock. By now, he knew from previous visits, the premises would be deserted but for the bored duty technician on the top floor, reading a magazine and chewing on a TV dinner while he waited for an emergency, which had never arisen—before tonight. Hankin rose, unbolted the door of the toilet, and crept softly into the carpeted corridor.

In an office whose door had been left ajar he spotted an Irish blackthorn walking stick in a big brass jug used as an umbrella stand. He hefted it as he tiptoed up the stairs to the top floor, not wanting to disturb the technician by using the local elevator and having its soft hum warn of his arrival. The stick seemed ideal for his purpose, and was; a single violent blow to the temple sent the man sprawling, unconscious in a gathering pool of his own blood.

With unhesitating swiftness, Hankin moved around the huge, bright hall from machine to machine, switching out every last one of the hundred-plus standard programs. Then he came to the specials—the ones for which psychiatrists had supplied the text for private recordings addressed to particular patients.

He smiled. There were dossiers in connection with each of the specials, and the dossiers included photos. The technician had not yet eaten his TV dinner, and it seemed a shame to waste it. Hankin sat down and munched reflectively as he leafed through the dossiers, stopping occasionally to impress a juicy detail on his mind and add it to the fund of ideas he had brought with him.

When he discovered the silvery-blond typist, about four hundred down from the head of the list, he put her dossier aside, making a note of its code number. Then he found scissors and a tape splicer, and set to work.

By eleven o'clock, which he had set as his deadline— that being the likely time for most of the clients to go to bed and switch on their Soundsleep equipment—he had reconnected all the standard programs to a set of tape loops recorded in his own voice. He had only had time to prepare about two dozen of these, but he had contrasted them as widely as possible.

They were in his own voice. That was what counted.

He tapped a switch and listened critically to the various orders he had recorded: "When you get up in the morning, don't put on your clothes. Go to the elevator and down to the street. Throw your arms around the first person you see and kiss him—or her—with passion. . ." "When you wake up, don't go to the bathroom. Go out on the street and do it there, in the gutter. . . ." "When you wake up, don't cook the eggs for breakfast. Go to the window overlooking the street and see how many people you can hit on the head with them. . ." "When you wake up, make a pile of the blankets in the middle of your bed and set a match to them. . ." "When you wake up, go straight to the garage and get out the car. Drive it as fast as you can in reverse gear along the wrong side of the street. . ." "When you wake up, don't go feed the baby. Fill a glass with your milk and try to sell it on the sidewalk outside. . . ."

He gave a satisfied nod and switched the machinery on. By noon tomorrow, Soundsleep Corporation would be destroyed.

He turned finally to the last special which he had retained from the total of two thousand-odd now receiving his own new "standard programs," and recorded a tape for the benefit of the little silvery-blond girl. He said in a perfectly matter-of-fact tone, "Get up right away, get dressed, come down to the Soundsleep building and make love to me."

He connected the tape to the output circuit, and yawned, and went to tie up the technician, who was now stirring and moaning faintly, so that this night, when he regained himself, should not be spoiled by the man's meddling.

THE WARP AND THE
WOOF-WOOF

A rabbit—even a dream rabbit—running through long grass ought not to make crunching noises like small stones being ground together. Which meant, Jeff decided, that he was being woken up.

Regretfully giving up the chase after the white bobtail, he stretched himself from the tip of his blunt nose to the end of his long and somewhat kinky tail, and grew aware of three things in quick succession. The first was an itch behind his ear, but that could be attended to later. The second was a savory smell in the room; even if it wasn't rabbit, it had possibilities. The third was that the crunching sounds were made by someone coming up the gravel path to the front door, who was now stopping and pushing a key into the lock. Master was home!

Jeff—who had been called Jeff for the good and sufficient reason that that was the next thing to a mutt—picked himself off the floor and threw himself bodily at Tom Halliday.

"Oof!" said his master explosively. "Get *down*, you preposterous beast!"

Jeff sat back on his haunches and looked up worriedly, giving the tip of his tail a tentative wag. Tom glared at him long enough to make his misshapen ears droop, and then grinned and rubbed the top of his head.

"You be careful!" he said. "You don't have to murder me to prove you're glad I'm here!"

Jeff gave one really frantic wag to show he understood, and followed his master as he went through the hall into the kitchen, doing his best not to knock over anything on the way. It was difficult, of course, because he was the kind of dog which is always too large for any room it is in—not a sensitive, snooty, pedigreed type of dog, but an accidentally evolved one who looked like a retriever from *this* angle and a sheepdog from *that* angle, with a touch of spaniel about the ears and a nose like a Stafford. He was, in fact, none of these; he was Jeff.

"Hullo, darling," said Susan Halliday without turning round from the stove. "That tickles, but I like it."

"Good," Tom answered, and reached past her to lift the lid on one of the pans. The smell suddenly redoubled, and Jeff gave a fairly quiet woof of joy on recognizing it.

"You shut up, Jeff," said Susan, poking him in the ribs with one small toe. "How did it go today, Tom honey?"

"Pretty hectic." Tom splashed water into the sink until it ran warm, and reached for the soap. "Ferris put me through the reaction tests again this morning, and I had another session in the G-chair this afternoon, and then Doc gave me the works. I didn't know one could feel naked inside as well as out till he started on me."

"And what did they say?"

Tom shot a sharp glance at his wife, but reached for the towel and dried his hands before answering. "They said I was in terrific shape."

"That's good," Susan said with forced brightness, and began to stir the contents of the pan. Jeff sensed that something must be wrong, and put out one immense forepaw to touch her leg. Barely in time he remembered that on the last occasion when he did that he ruined something called "a perfectly-good-pair-stockings"; he changed his mind and merely whimpered.

For a second Tom hesitated. Then he tossed the towel over the back of a handy chair and crossed the floor to put his hands on Susan's shoulders, turning her around gently. He said, "Darling, why don't you say it straight out—that you don't want me to go?"

She pulled away from him and looked down at the stove. "Of course I don't, honey," she said huskily. "But of course, I *do*—because you want to, and I know how much it means to you, and I know what a happy, wonderful sort of person you're going to be when you come back to me. . . . But I can't help it if I'm afraid for you, Tom!"

"There's nothing to be afraid of," Tom said comfortingly. "Robot rockets have done the round trip, landed and come back safely—there's no reason why a rocket carrying a man instead of machinery shouldn't do the same. I've been up to the moon twice, and you didn't object then."

"But the moon's different! Lots of people have been to the moon, and anyway it's all barren, no air or anything. But on Mars—well, just suppose that . . ."

"Martians you mean?" A slow grin broke out across Tom's face. "Martian monsters? You've been watching too many teleshows, my sweet! I wondered what could have got at you!"

"But—" Susan began defensively, and got no further before she found that Tom's grin was infectious. Well, really it was rather ridiculous; she couldn't keep from an answering smile, and then they broke out laughing together.

Jeff, realizing that whatever had been making his owners unhappy was over with, got up from the floor and did his personal dance of joy. Somehow or other he managed to knock over a chair almost at once, and when he backed hastily away to avoid it, his tail wreaked considerable havoc among pans racked under the sink.

"Sometimes," Tom said when the last echoes of the crash had died away, "I'm very glad Jeff has no dachshund in his family tree."

"How do you mean?" Susan said, wiping her eyes.

"Think how much extra trouble it would be," Tom answered as he bent to clear the mass, "if we had to go into the next room to pick up the things he'd knocked over."

Jr-Ktuk had never seen a teleshow, and therefore had no prejudices about Martian monsters. He was quite content to *be* one: pseudopods, palpitating brain case, sixteen eyes and all. At the moment twelve of his eyes were registering expressions of mingled astonishment, disbelief and dismay, and the remainder were studying Ol-Pshok as though he were a singularly unpleasant sandlouse.

"*What* did you say?" he demanded. He had heard quite well, but he had so many eyes expressing incredulity that he thought he'd better make certain.

Ol-Pshok was patently very flustered. To gain time, he embarked on a complicated obeisance which would have taken him the best part of four days if he had completed it, but Jr-Ktuk was in no mood to squat on ceremony. He cut short the bow after less than three hours with an impatient wave of a pseudopod. "Speak up!" he ordered.

"Well," Ol-Pshok resumed obediently, "as you know, a year ago we were again scheduled to reconnoiter the surface of our planet on the off chance that it had returned to habitable condition. The odds against such an occurrence are, of course, tremendous, but the caves in which we have been compelled to reside for the past ninety-six and one-third generations induce a certain claustrophobia which the excursions to the surface tend to ameliorate—"

Belatedly Jr-Ktuk recognized the opening of the first indoctrination lecture to the young, which a fast talker had trouble in delivering in under thirty-nine hours, and gave vent to a bellow of annoyance. Ol-Pshok disappeared automatically behind the nearest boulder, while Jr-Ktuk muttered some pointed remarks about the drawbacks of promoting a pedagogue to the post of Chief Assistant, no matter how distinguished his academic career.

With commendable restraint he tore off only three of Ol-Pshok's pseudopods before he calmed down, but all his eyes showed impatience when he said, "This is your last chance, Ol-Pshok! *Get—to—the—point!*"

Since each word of the last sentence was emphasized by a bang of his head against the rocky wall, Ol-Pshok could not help but nod agreement. "Very well, then," said Jr-Ktuk, relenting a little.

"When we were surveying the ninety-fourth quadrant," Ol-Pshok stated comparatively baldly, "we found a rocket-propelled vehicle parked on a sand flat. It was apparently under remote control, since while we watched it took off again and entered an orbit which seemed to be aimed at—" He paused impressively for effect, and Jr-Ktuk was sufficiently shaken by the information so far to let the silence last for all of an hour and a quarter before he made an ominous move.

"—Earth!" finished Ol-Pshok just in time, waggling all available pseudopods with suppressed excitement.

"Oh, no!" said Jr-Ktuk from the bottom of his cardio-vascular system.

"Oh, yes!" contradicted Ol-Pshok, greatly daring. "Definitely yes!"

"Anything else?" Nine of Jr-Ktuk's eyes showed deep concentration, and Ol-Pshok was startled. It was commonly known in the caves that Jr-Ktuk was too vain about his ratiocinatory faculties ever to allow anyone to see that a problem engaged more than a fraction of his attention. Nine-sixteenths was a new high.

But the baleful glare of the remaining seven eyes soon recalled him to his purpose.

"Er—yes," he went on hastily. "We found traces of five similar landings in the recent past. Our psychostatisticians, whose function as predictors of—"

Something warned him just in time that his enthusiasm for the ninth basic indoctrination lecture had better not run away with him. "Well, anyway, they tell me that it looks very much as though the Earthmen have got air current of our plan to take over their planet and have decided to strike before us." As Jr-Ktuk had feared, he automatically added the associated platitude. "Eight-tentacled is it whose cause is just, but sixteen it who gets its blow in fust."

"Enough!" snarled Jr-Ktuk. "But that reminds me. I haven't had a report from the Invasion Department for two and a half generations now. Who's in charge of the department at the moment?"

"I am," said Ol-Pshok, with more than a trace of pride.

That was too much.

When Jr-Ktuk had finished burying the remains, he stuck a pseudopod down the communications aperture in the wall of the throne cave, and sent for Wy-Thob, formerly deputy chief and now full chief of the Invasion Department. He liked Wy-Thob considerably more than he had liked Ol-Pshok, and therefore waited with only a little bad grace while Wy-Thob performed the six-day-long wave of farewell over his predecessor's grave.

"Now," said Jr-Ktuk when the formality was over, "how about a progress report? And remember: Ol-Pshok's worst fault was taking his time."

"Things aren't so dusty," the new department chief said. "As a matter of fact, Tlo-Krog tipped me the closing of half his eyes about this missile from Earth, so I ordered a reconnaissance to find out what the Earthmen were actually up to. We only finished it three months ago, but the information is already on the way to you."

"Fast work," said Jr-Ktuk approvingly. "What did you find?"

"They don't apparently plan a full-scale invasion yet. They've gone to a great deal of trouble to prepare a being called Tomalliday for the job. Odd names the Earthmen give themselves," he added in passing, and Jr-Ktuk frowned. Only in the job for a couple of weeks, and here he was developing the habit of wandering off down side-tracks instead of sticking to the point at issue.

"However," pursued Wy-Thob, oblivious of the risk he was running, "we've established this being's location, and we know he's the only one they intend to send here."

"By rocket, I suppose," said Jr-Ktuk musingly.

"Of course." Wy-Thob looked reminiscent with three of his eyes. "You know, it's just as well the Earthmen haven't discovered the spacewarp, or they'd have overrun us already. It's so much easier to send something away from the sun—downhill, as you might say—but as for the other direction . . . well, as you know, we've been working on the invasion problem for sixty-three generations without getting anywhere, least of all to Earth." He chuckled with all his mouths at once, which was abominably bad manners in the presence of a superior, and Jr-Ktuk tore off two of his pseudopods as punishment. Slightly chastened, Wy-Thob went on—as soon as he could.

"As I was saying, the Earthmen are very close to achieving their object."

"But they're sending only one being?" Jr-Ktuk pressed. Wy-Thob signified assent.

"Fine!" said Jr-Ktuk energetically. "You will arrange to spacewarp him here. The loss of the being they have trained for the trip will subject them to delay and give your department an inhaling space in which to produce the results your late, unlamented predecessor did not get."

Wy-Thob turned maroon with astonishment, but Jr-Ktuk pursued relentlessly, "In order to make certain nothing goes wrong, I propose to supervise the operation my-self. Come on!"

Following his superior out of the throne cave at a

respectful distance, Wy-Thob was thoughtful. He had long ago come to the conclusion that, since the only possible reason for invading another planet was to dispossess the original owners and since the Earthmen were only planning to send a single individual in their rocket, they must be certain that one of their kind could handle the whole job. Consequently attendance at the opening of a warp containing that Earthman would be dangerous. He said nothing, chiefly because prior to the decease of Ol-Pshok he had been six hundred and eighth in line for Jr-Ktuk's job, whereas now he was six hundred and seventh. The future looked rosy.

Jr-Ktuk was obviously going through one of his periods of self-abnegation, because they ran all the way from the throne cave to the Invasion Department on the other side of the planet, arriving less than a month later. The business of setting up the warp was easy; they had so many machines arranged to send Martians to Earth—which was impossible—that they could have spared dozens of them to be reversed. One was all they needed for Jr-Ktuk's plan. Barely three days after their arrival Wy-Thob cleared most of his throats and began.

"We have established," he said in a didactic tone of voice that made Jr-Ktuk look at him sharply to be sure it was he and not Ol-Pshok speaking, "that the being called Tomalliday is located at this point." He used five pseudopods to indicate appropriate five-dimensional coordinates. "The machine is set to transfer the living being of maximum intelligence located within a certain radius of that point. The materialization will occur on that bench of rock over there. It is protected by glass, so there's no need to worry."

Jr-Ktuk nodded his approval, and Wy-Thob jabbed the technician squatting at the controls in the large of his back. "You may start the process now," he said.

The complicated warp machinery began to glow and hiss and spit, and Jr-Ktuk watched it. Believing that his chief's attention was fully occupied, Wy-Thob started to edge for the exit.

"*Where* do you think you're going?" said Jr-Ktuk sternly, reaching out a pseudopod so long he would surely have torn it off a subordinate. Since he was junior to no one, he could extrude it with impunity.

"Oh—well—" hedged Wy-Thob, realizing too late that Jr-Ktuk's reputation for multiple attention was well-founded, "I was—uh—that is, check the power supply . . ."

Jr-Ktuk subjected him to a withering glare from all his eyes. There was a short pause of an hour or two. Finally he spoke.

"How large a radius is your machine set for, Wy-Thob?" he asked in a dreadfully silky tone. "How big, in other words, is this Earthman?"

In spite of knowing what he was in for, Wy-Thob flinched when he glanced at the materialization bench. He calmed himself with an effort.

"L-look for yourself!" he suggested, waving a pseudo-pod at the alien which had just arrived. Jr-Ktuk spared one eye to do so.

The shock was so great that he involuntarily brought all his eyes to bear a moment later, and Wy-Thob, ultramarine with relief, seized his chance to break the current record for the distance between himself and the door, leaving the hapless technician and Jr-Ktuk to face the danger on their own.

There was a long silence. Then Jr-Ktuk remembered that he was supposed to set an example. White-carapaced, he said, "What—a—*monster!*"

"This has been a lovely evening, darling," said Susan Halliday, snuggling up to her husband as they walked along the path toward their bungalow. "Hurry up back so we can do it again."

Tom slid his key into the lock of the front door. "Trust me, my sweet. I'm not going chasing after any lush Martian princesses when I have you to come home to."

She smiled sleepily. "I can hardly believe it's tomorrow you're leaving. Hasn't the time flown?"

Tom's eyes went up to the tiny, racing star overhead which was the launching station. In the same orbit was the ship which would carry him to Mars. He said, "But aren't you glad the psychologists said we could carry on a normal life together till the last day? Instead of my having to be treated like a lab specimen, the way it used to happen?"

"Mmm!" said Susan, and took his hand to draw him into the dark hallway. "Hullo!" she added a moment later. "Where's Jeff?"

"Dreaming about rabbits, I guess," Tom answered lightly. "Jeff! Here, boy—we're home!"

There was silence.

"That's odd," said Susan. "Did you shut the back door?"

"I think so." Tom went forward and turned on the light in the kitchen. After a moment he called back, "Yes, it's shut. And I closed the windows before we went out. Is he on our bed?"

"Oh, not Jeff!" said Susan. But she went to look all the same.

He wasn't on the bed. He wasn't on the sofa in the lounge, and he wasn't hiding because he'd misbehaved himself, or if he had, he'd done it somewhere where they couldn't find it.

"Ah, well," said Tom finally, dismissing it. "He's too clever by half. He must have managed to get out somehow and go chasing cats. He had his collar on, and somebody will find him and get him back to us. Come on, darling—don't worry."

Rabbits, decided Jeff, even in dreams, don't make high-pitched squeaking noises. Only mice do that, and if he was going to dream about chasing mice, he might as well see what turning over would do for him. Mice weren't worth the effort, even in dreams—they were too small and too agile to catch.

He opened one eye lazily, giving his tail a brief wag for luck in case what had disturbed him had been his owners' coming home. Then he forgot all his manners and scrambled to his feet, legs and tail flying in all directions. This wasn't his home!

To start with, the light was wrong—dim and reddish. And the walls should have been straight up and down, not curved as if they had been scraped out underground. For a moment he was afraid that he was having a nightmare about being stuck down a rabbit hole, but there was nothing rabbity about this place. It didn't smell right at all.

But it smelled good.

He wagged his tail and thereby demolished a bank of fragile equipment. The noise startled him, and he half expected to hear his master scold him for being a clumsy brute. Nothing happened.

After a while he remembered that he hadn't stretched on waking up, so he did, and the glass surrounding the ledge of rock on which he stood proved unequal to the strain. It gave with a crash, and on turning one astonished eye toward the source of the noise, he saw something move. More puzzled than ever, he extended his neck and snuffed at it.

It wasn't a mouse. On one or two occasions he had gotten close enough to mice to see what they looked like. This object was about the same size, true, but its smell reminded him of the crumbs of cheese he was sometimes given off the dinner table at home. He loved cheese, but the Hallidays would never give him as much as he wanted. He put out the red rag of a tongue.

Yes, *very* like cheese. He licked again. The second time was more than Jr-Ktuk could stand, and he did the only thing a good Martian ruler could do. He ran.

Not so nippy as mice, either, thought Jeff with satisfaction, putting down one of his ungainly forepaws on top of Jr-Ktuk's yell. This looked promising.

When he had finished Jr-Ktuk—who tasted *exactly* like cheese, except for the hard bits, which he left—he got down from the ledge and snuffed around. He was sure he had seen two of the cheese creatures, but the other one had gone.

The warp machinery attracted his notice. He snuffed at it, decided there was one thing wrong with it, and put that right after the manner of dogs. He suffered a small electric shock in the process, so he trod on it to teach it better.

Then he snuffed along the trail left by the one that got away, and it led him to a gap in the wall which was too small for his body by nine-tenths. But the earth around it yielded to his experimental scraping, and he gave himself up to the task of excavation with a small wuff of pure joy.

Even in his wildest dreams he had never come up with anything like this. To be chasing mice that weren't fast enough to get away, and that tasted like cheese when they were caught, through something similar to an endless rabbit burrow, was to Jeff a good preview of heaven.

A long time later a rather swollen Jeff struggled out of the surface entrance of one of the caves and looked about him, panting. The technician who got away had spread the news through the tunnels that there was a monster from Earth on the rampage, and so many of the Martians had been able to take to their own personal escape routes—some into the past, some into other dimensions, and most of them into refuges that they themselves didn't understand. They were now kicking themselves (which, with their number of legs, was quite a painful process) for not finding out about this before, instead of wasting time in stuffy caves on a dying planet. Nonetheless, Jeff had persuaded quite a few of them to remain behind.

His heaven, though, was wearing thin. He had eaten so much that he had been having to make his holes larger than usual, and he was coming to realize that, with their usual remarkable wisdom and ineffable perspicacity, his owners had been right to stop him from eating too much cheese. He burped frequently and was beginning to feel queasy.

Wanting to express his feelings in the most sublime and artistic manner open to him, he scrambled up to the top of a little ridge nearby, wriggled his haunches into the dusty soil, and threw back his head to howl.

The first sounds died in his throat as he suddenly took in something he hadn't noticed before. Then he closed his eyes, an expression of doggy ecstasy on his face which not even his indigestion could dim. This was almost too much.

Two moons to bay at!

And his master was coming.

THE PRODUCT OF
THE MASSES

The mutual attraction between two bodies
is proportional to the product of their masses and
inversely proportional to the distance between them.
—FOLK SAYING, BELIEVED PREATOMIC

"Is anything the matter?" Dr. Leila Kunje inquired coolly when Jeff Hook had been staring into the transpex bubble for a good half-minute or more. It contained—a creature. A creature whose dark gray, flattened-disc body was suspended from a frame like the ribs of an umbrella and surrounded by more legs than any beast had a right to own if it were larger than a millipede. This thing was a good sixty feet overall.

In addition, its hide hung on it like an ill-fitting flour sack, patched with flakes the colors of mildew, gangrene and rust. That was what was riveting Jeff's attention: the half-formed question of how something so deformed and leprous could survive.

He tore his eyes away and fixed them instead on what ought to have been, but for some unaccountable reason was not, a far more inviting prospect—the xenobiologist at his side.

"I was just impressing the details on my memory," he lied, then added because he was unsure how well he had concealed his reaction, "It's not a very prepossessing beast, is it?"

"On the contrary," Dr. Kunje said. "It—or to be more exact, *she*—is an exceptionally well-endowed specimen."

"She?"

"We decided on a female because they are somewhat larger than the males, which gives us additional space inside the carcass, naturally, and also because of the relative territorial habits of the two sexes. The females tend to stay in any given area for a fairly long time, whereas the males roam from place to place. At the stage our survey has now reached, we are adequately supplied with the kind of superficial data that can be gathered from a hasty once-over. What we need is the fine detail to complete the picture. Do you follow me?" Dr. Kunje spoke with the politely patronizing tone of the expert forced to enlist the aid of a handyman for a relatively insignificant task.

Jeff gave her the same kind of thoughtful examination he had given the creature in the bubble, and noted a remarkable parallel between her and it. She was—if he wasn't mistaken—potentially a rather beautiful woman: tall, with dark hair and large, bright eyes, and a tawny-gold complexion. But, as though to deny any continuity between the part of her that was exposed and the part that was covered, she chose to wear the loosest and baggiest set of all-purpose coveralls he had ever seen, and furthermore to string them about and stuff their pockets with whatever could be called on to provide lumps and bulges in the wrong places.

He felt a vague stir of disappointment. The universe was awfully big, and the tiny enclaves of human awareness that were the starships, darting from system to system, were oppressively small. They far too easily became boring, and though he had an excellent and reliable crew working under him, he could tell that he was near his own personal limit of endurance and might soon start to snap at those he was really most fond of. He had looked forward to this unexpected assignment, calling at the Chryseis research station and helping out with a key project, mainly as a chance to renew his sense of . . . what would you call it? Solidarity? That feeling of companionship, at any rate, which alone sustained wandering humanity among these harsh stars and bleak, uninhabitable planets.

Granted, research scientists were of a different temperament from people who went into the Advance Guard. Nonetheless, they also being human—

"You do an awful lot of staring, Commander Hook!" Dr. Kunje said sharply.

"I find you much more enjoyable to look at than the

creature in there," Jeff said, with a jerk of his thumb toward the bubble. It was a compliment honestly enough meant, but the response it provoked was the freezing of her dark eyes into chips of black Plutonian ice.

"You are not here to enjoy anything, Commander!" the xenobiologist said. "You are here to perform a service for us. Can it be done?"

"I guess so," Jeff sighed, and turned to go. When he was twenty paces distant along the tunnel that linked the bubble with the main section of the orbital research station, she called after him.

"By the way, Commander!"

"Yes?"

"Your—shall we say, politely, 'uncalled-for'?—remark just now reminded me of a point I had been intending to bring to your attention. I know that the members of the Guards lead a somewhat irregular life during their long periods on patrol, but that is perhaps excusable in view of the shortage of genuinely demanding tasks they are called on to fulfill. I should just like to make it plain that here we do have such tasks—any number of them—and I have no intention of permitting the *looseness* of your customary behavior to contaminate my staff."

Jeff, struggling through the haze of verbiage, gave a blank headshake.

"I'm telling you, Commander," Dr. Kunje said in an impatient tone, "to keep fraternization to a minimum during your stay. Do you understand, or must I draw you physiological diagrams?"

When he reentered the lock of his own ship, Jeff found two of the research station staff already present, talking with his senior lieutenants: a large, stout, motherly, fair-haired woman of early middle age whom he identified from the records he had studied on the way here as Dr. Ingrid Swann, and a younger man, very lean and nervous but affable in manner, whom he recognized as Dr. Matthew Couperin.

Lieutenant Sandy Baravitch was talking as he came in—she had probably been doing most of the talking, as usual—but she broke off in mid-sentence and blew him a kiss of welcome.

"How did you get on with the dragon?" she exclaimed.

Beside her, Lieutenant Tom Cheliki winced and glanced at the strangers, his protuberant eyes very bright in his dark face, but the stout woman gave a wry chuckle.

"Please don't judge all of us by Dr. Kunje!" she said. "It simply wouldn't be fair."

"That's good," Jeff sighed, and slumped into a vacant chair at the projector table, on which the scientists were displaying the data concerning their venture. There were four half-empty glasses apparently balanced on treetops in a Chryseian jungle, and he brightened at the sight of them.

"One for you?" Sandy suggested, and suited the action to the word by reaching toward the refreshment dispenser.

"I've just been sternly warned against this sort of behavior," Jeff said. "No fraternizing, to quote the exact phrase."

"You must be joking!" Tom said. "This is our first outship contact in over four months, and for these poor so-and-so's it's the first in—how long did you say, Matt?"

Dr. Couperin stared briefly at the ceiling. "Ah . . . eight months, four days and sixteen minutes, to the moment your commander stepped through our lock."

Having lowered the level in his glass by a conservative fifty percent, Jeff set it down along with the others, on the crown of a remarkably Earthlike tree. "I get the impression that Dr. Kunje likes it that way. What's wrong? Has she been crossed in love or something?"

"Don't be unkind to her," Ingrid Swann said. "She's an absolutely first-class biologist, and it's something of an honor for us to be working under her."

"What she needs is someone to get to work on top of her," Couperin said, barely audibly, and then flushed bright red as he turned to Sandy. "I'm sorry, that was unspeakably crude! It just slipped out."

But Sandy was grinning so broadly that the freckles on her cheeks had almost disappeared into a succession of dimples. She reached over and patted Couperin's hand.

"That's okay! So long as somebody retains a sense of humor here, I guess we can bear to stick around long enough to do the job your boss wants from us. Jeff, did you get all the details, or do you want us to run through them again?"

"To be frank, I cut my interview with Dr. Kunje short," Jeff admitted. "Let's take it again from the top. There was one question in particular I didn't get around to asking, and I should have done. I gather that Chryseis is pretty well a terra-type world, correct?"

Ingrid nodded.

"In other words, it has CHON-type biology—carbon, hydrogen, oxygen, nitrogen—fairly standard gravity, regular proportions of land to ocean, same general temperature and so forth. Well, in the past century or so we must have run across fifty or sixty worlds of this type. What's so special about Chryseis that it's attracted a research team like yours, and that it rates a priority adequate to haul an Advance Guard boat off its routine patrol and enlist our help?"

Couperin leaned forward so that he appeared to be resting his elbows on the treetops within the projector table. "My best guess is a sense of racial guilt," he said.

"What?"

"Let's look at it this way. What were the largest animals ever to exist on Earth?"

Jeff hesitated. "Why . . . well, some species of dinosaur, I imagine. Probably *Diplodocus*."

"Wrong. He wasn't the biggest, just the longest. The biggest creatures ever to appear on Earth were the giant whales, and we exterminated them around the beginning of the twenty-first century." Couperin hunched a little farther over the table. "A couple of decades before we developed skills in biology adequate to find out what made them tick, genetically and otherwise, and preserve them in the new, inhospitable, made-over environment we'd wished on them. They weren't simply hunted to death, though that did reduce the numbers far enough to allow them to give in to the other factors that were operating. Effectively, we poisoned them, and when they were weakened by poison, disease did the rest.

"Right now, life here on Chryseis is going through a phase of extreme gigantism. It's the first world of its kind we've run across, and it's astonishingly close to Earth in so many chemical ways it holds the promise of millions of valuable clues to what we lost at home just before we learned to comprehend it. Tom, flip back to shot nineteen, will you?"

Tom Cheliki operated the projector table's control dial and the scene changed. Now it showed a patch of ground with low-growing bushes and a scrawny reptilian creature browsing among them.

Jeff looked down obediently, but after a moment shrugged.

"That little baby," Couperin said didactically, "corresponds to a rat in Earthside ecology, very nearly. It's a little over ten feet tall."

"What?"

"No kidding, Commander. I said, and I mean, *extreme* gigantism. Didn't you see Dr. Kunje's pride and joy?"

"The disguise, floating in the transpex bubble?"

"Precisely. Except that 'stalking-horse' would be a better term. That's an exact replica of—Tom, give us shot sixty-three, please!"

The scene is the table changed again; this time it showed a typical specimen of the genus Jeff had already seen, indistinguishable apart from the different distribution of the colored patches on its body and legs.

"We studied five or six hundred examples of *Macrodiscos polychromia chryseiana*," Ingrid explained, "and derived a computer-analyzed cross section of it, to incorporate every known characteristic: the appearance, the mode of gait, the general behavior, the smell it emits, even. Then we programmed for a carcass matching the description, with space inside it for one standard Advance Guard landing globe. The idea being—"

"The idea being," Couperin cut in, "that Dr. Kunje is fanatically opposed to *anything,* no matter how slight, that might interfere with the habits of the species under observation. This whole job could easily be done with our own resources, by dropping remotes to the surface. But oh, no! Dr. Kunje insists that the *Macrodiscoi* be observed at first hand by something that will pass as one of their own number."

"Tell me something," Jeff said suddenly. "Do you never refer to your boss except as *Doctor* Kunje?"

The two scientists exchanged glances. After a moment, they both shook their heads.

"Good grief," Jeff said, wondering what it would be like to try and cope with his twelve-member crew on a basis of heel-clicking and cries of *Sah!* instead of laughter, dirty jokes and a great many displays of overt affection. He was brought back from his fit of speculation by Sandy playing footsy with him under the table, and cleared his throat.

"Ah—*yes!* Well, assuming the program for the stalking-horse included the proper specifications for implanting the landingglobe inside it, I don't see why it shouldn't work. There's certainly plenty of room—one of our globes is approximately twenty-seven feet across with the force shield in full operation."

"Dr. Kunje was very thorough about that," Ingrid said. "You have to give her that: she's always thorough. And the form of the *Macrodiscos* luckily lends itself to the plan. The generators are at the top of the globe, right? And the beastie is more or less suspended from a frame of bone with the nerve tissues running along the—ah—the ribs. But you've seen the actual model we're going to use, so I don't have to explain in detail."

"So the generators can plug directly into the nervous system." Jeff nodded. "That's neat. And I assume you have a program of operation we can simply slot into our own computers?"

"Exactly."

"I see. Tom, toss me the dial, will you?" Jeff reached out for the projector-table controls, and wiped the shot currently on display. "So it's going to go like this," he continued, frowning a little because some of the details were still rather hazy, and manipulated the image within the table until it suggested, at least in outline, one of the *Macrodiscoi*. Into the middle of it, with the greater ease of long familiarity, he injected one of the Guard's landing globes: the central shaft first, housing the power sources (tripled against emergency), then the three levels around which the shield projectors radiated blurred streaks of warning red, the uppermost housing weaponry, the central one available for observation, and the lowermost forming the most perfect extension of human reason yet devised, being as it was one huge solid-state computer into which the globe's crew could directly plug themselves simply by laying their hands flat on the contact plates before their chairs. Doing that was an eerie sensation, but it had its rewards; that, truly, was an extension of consciousness, and he had sometimes suspected that a kind of addiction to it was what kept him on in the Advance Guard, trespassing on planet after inhospitable planet.

He was rather proud of his ability to sketch with the unprogrammed controls of the projector table. He added some fine touches to his drawing—a recognizable caricature of Dr. Kunje, for example, on the middle level, peering out with one hand raised to shade her eyes.

"Don't take all *day*, will you?" Sandy said caustically, and he caught himself with a guilty start. Trying to look as though nothing had happened, he removed his glass—which was now balanced on top of a peculiarly nasty little weapon built into the upper level of the globe—and reduced its contents to nil.

"Is that the general idea?" he asked Ingrid.

"Yes, that's fine," she said after a few seconds' contemplation. "I take it that means it can be done."

"Oh, sure!"

"Jeff, just a second," Sandy said, frowning now as she stared into the table. "Matthew, this is the boss species here—correct?"

"No, not exactly," Couperin countered. "There are several others more widely spread over the planet, but this is by far the largest."

"How far is 'far'?"

"Ten or fifteen percent."

"And what kind of terrain are we going to have to work over when we go down?" Sandy glanced up at him. "I don't think I told you, but I'm supposed to be the planetside pilot for this crew, which means that, whenever we discharge a landing globe, I'm responsible."

"I'll show you." Couperin turned to Jeff. "Ah—Commander, do you mind if I wipe this drawing?"

"Sure, sure! I only wanted to be certain I had the picture firmly in my mind. You needn't bother to store it." Jeff passed over the control unit for the table. "And, by the way, stop calling me 'Commander.' I've decided I won't take that kind of language from anyone except Dr. Kunje."

Couperin looked briefly puzzled, then smiled. He dialed for another picture, and the table produced a revolving globe of Chryseis.

"Here's the territory where the *Macrodiscoi* hang out," he said. A patch on one of the northern land masses flickered white. "As you probably know, the year here is about seventeen months long, and the northern winter is just about ending now. The preliminary surveys caught the broad outline of the species' summer habits, and we arrived in time to follow through their winter behavior in outline also. What we now want is the—"

"Don't tell me," Jeff cut in. "The fine detail. I get it. So what's the lay of the land like, and will you have another drink? Sandy!"

"Mainly savannah. These creatures are herbivorous—oh, thanks very much, I will." Couperin accepted his new drink and took a healthy swig. "Hah! Thank you. This is a very pleasant change from the monotonous stuff we get here."

"You get monotonous diets and liquors?" Tom Cheliki said disbelievingly.

"Liquors we get none of," Ingrid said. "It's—ah—not approved. Also, it conduces to lax behavior. Not that one really *needs* to be conduced, of course, because hormones are by far the most potent substances yet devised to affect human instincts. *But.*"

"I'm glad we called," Jeff said after a moment of blank astonishment, and everyone burst out laughing.

"Jeff, if you don't mind?" Sandy said, recovering before the others, and on his shrug continued: "This terrain, then! You say savannah? Any—oh—spring tornadoes? Earthquakes? Major risks of that kind?"

"No, it's a pretty hospitable world," Ingrid said. "We have the weather pattern down in detail, and it doesn't include anything worse than the occasional gale. But calling this simply savannah is simplifying it a bit. There are rocky patches, and even some stretches of fairly respectable forest. No tectonic activity worth mentioning in the range the *Macrodiscoi* cover, though there's a young continent emerging to the south—that one—and we have noted some fairly fierce temblors in the ridge of the east. However—"

"*Commander!*"

The word splashed into the room like a rock tossed into wet mud, and they all winced and turned toward the entrance. Dr. Kunje stood there, eyes once more like black ice chips, but this time blazing.

"Commander, I did not expect to have to gloss my instructions with this kind of detail, but I heard bawdy laughter echoing up the tube connecting this ship with the research station, and I thought I had better see what caused such unseemly merriment. And what do I find? I find that I should have spelled out my distaste at the idea of any of my staff taking drugs!"

She pointed a shaking finger at the glass Jeff was holding. "That does, does it not, contain *alcohol?*"

"Why, yes," Jeff said. Denials seemed superfluous. "Mine contains an exact simulacrum of Polish vodka. Would you care for something?"

For long moments Dr. Kunje was speechless. Then, at last and painfully, she forced out, "I shall be *so glad* when this experience is over! And, believe me, I no longer think it was a good idea to enlist the help of the Advance Guard in a purely scientific project!"

She spun on her heel and marched away. The sound of her heels could be heard fading as she stamped along the gravity plates lining the floor of the umbilical tunnel.

Eventually Jeff said, "I seem to have put you in dutch with your boss, don't I?"

"Well, we do have to survive here for another three months minimum," Couperin said, dutifully setting aside his glass, still three-quarters full.

"What's wrong with that woman?" Sandy burst out. "I understood she was a good biologist—doesn't she know anything about the chemical side of human behavior?"

"That, no," Ingrid said, and gave her habitual wry chuckle, which made her plump body shake clear down to her calves. "We have a theory that she was fathered by a computer. Matt worked out the physical details if you'd be interested?"

"Oh, lovely!" Sandy exploded, planting both elbows on

the projector table, details of the terrain on Chryseis forgotten. "Do tell!"

"Well, you see, it occurred to some of us that nobody with normal metabolism could be so utterly and entirely frigid," Ingrid said. "So—oh, Matt, you take it from there. You worked out the program."

Couperin looked vaguely uncomfortable. "It's just a gag," he said defensively. "But if you really want to know about it . . . ? Well, I started by considering the subjective aspect, corresponding to signals generated in the human nervous system, if a computer of, say, quarter-megabrain capacity were connected . . ."

When he finished, they were almost helpless with laughter; only Jeff retained a modicum of self-control, and he used it to shut the baffles in the umbilical tube and cut off the leakage of sound into the research station.

"It's practically literal!" Ingrid said, when she recovered from her hysteria. "Why . . . why, just to take one example, Dr. Kunje doesn't even like to refer to the tubes that you use to link ships in orbit as 'umbilical'! It brings to mind a process she'd rather forget about, even if the image is an exact one."

"But somebody like that is sick!" Tom Cheliki said, his mirth forgotten in an instant.

"In what sense?" Couperin countered. "She runs a first-rate station, there's no denying. And she has the best record in xenobiology anyone could hope to stack up in a lifetime."

"She's not functioning as a person, though," Sandy said soberly. They were all suddenly not amused. "Jeff?"

As commander of the Advance Guard ship, whose crew had to work in isolation for months at a time on the very fringes of human-explored space, and often had to risk their lives on strange planets with no more reward than the occasional use of the consciousness-expanding facilities of a landing globe, Jeff had to be both a theoretical and a practical psychologist. He said after a pause for reflection, "Yes, Sandy, I'm afraid you're absolutely right."

"What sustains someone in that predicament?" Tom Cheliki demanded. The two scientists, strangers to the close, almost telepathic unity of a Guard ship's crew, stared in bewilderment, feeling that some conclusion had been reached which they did not know about.

It had.

"Being right," Sandy said positively. "That so, Jeff?"

"Yes. And there comes a time when the personality is stretched like a rubber band—gets caught up in a Zeno race. The tortoise never does beat Achilles, even if the logic says it does."

"What's a Zeno race?" Ingrid demanded.

"What your boss is trapped in." Jeff shook himself, as though coming back to the present from a long way off—and that also was partly true. "Someone who is not operating as a normal person can only be operating in accordance with a false idea of a normal person. That false idea is what we nickname a Zeno race. You know the paradox of Achilles and the tortoise! When the tortoise has gone such a distance, Achilles starts to run, but when he gets to where the tortoise was when he started, it has moved on, and then when he—"

"Sure!" Couperin said impatiently.

"Well, someone who has to be right in order to survive as a thinking person isn't normal, is he—or she? Most human beings are wrong part of the time. Someone who depends on being right is trapped in a paradox like Zeno's, *having* to be right and each time finding it more difficult to make it there ahead of the crowd. In fact, there always comes a time when the paradox resolves. And unless I'm mistaken, your boss just passed it.

"*Snap.*"

Puzzled, Ingrid said, "But—"

"It's just as well she called us in to lend you a landing globe!" Tom Cheliki said, his dark face drawn and worried. "You might not have spotted it. What do we do, Jeff?"

"We let her be wrong." Jeff shrugged and leaned back in his seat, cradling his drink. "What's more, I think she's already left out of account the factor which is going to demonstrate that she *can* be wrong. Ingrid, didn't you say something about your having been here throughout the period of winter on the *Macrodiscoi*'s range?"

"Why, yes!"

"You'll have to edit me a bit, because I'm not sufficiently

grounded in xenobiology to know if the basic assumption is sound, but I suspect that, when we put our landing globe inside your stalking horse and go down, the following will . . ."

"Now, this is going to be perfectly straightforward," Dr. Kunje said as she faced the assembled crew of the landing globe: half members of the Guard, half members of her own staff with specific tasks to attend to during the descent and the stay on the surface. "Our surroundings may be unfamiliar, but our purpose is what it always is on visiting a new planet: to gather knowledge."

She glanced about her rather uneasily, as though oppressed by the blackness beyond the limits of the globular shield protecting them. Outside was the incredible, internal nakedness of the facsimile *Macrodiscos* they had built, its circulation, musculature and in fact every other organ but the digestive system plainly visible, pushed into curious new relationships by the presence of the globe in place of the intestine equivalents. Their stalking-horse would even be able to breathe, to economize on the power sources within the globe, which were not designed to make sixty-odd tons of alien protoplasm gallop across a grassy plain at forty miles an hour.

"Finished?" Sandy said briskly from the control console. "Good! Here we go!"

And, permitting just a shade of acceleration to leak through the shield—enough to jar Dr. Kunje on her feet and interrupt her declaration that she had barely started to deliver her speech—she launched her weird craft into atmosphere. Outside the globe: the *Macrodiscos*. Outside the *Macrodiscos*: a shield unit to absorb and dissipate the friction from diving through air a trifle thicker than Earth's, plus a computer with a single program and a homing device with a million-mile range. If something were to go wrong with the plan, they could abandon the carcass they hid inside and signal the external shield unit to come and fetch them, fast.

Not that Dr. Kunje was expecting any such eventuality; as she had stressed over and over again, their stalking-horse and the program that was operating it was squarely founded on months of careful study of the *Macrodiscoi* and related species.

But Jeff was.

Keeping his hands dutifully linked in his lap—no one but Sandy was supposed to touch the contact plates until she had set them safely on solid ground—he glanced at Dr. Kunje in the adjacent chair.

"Excited, Doctor?" he suggested, noting how white her knuckles were from tension.

"Why—yes, I suppose I am," Dr. Kunje admitted, with a trace of condescension. "It's always most gratifying to see the culmination of a long plan of action working out exactly as predicted, isn't it?"

Jeff kept his thoughts on the subject to himself, and merely gave her an apparently confirmatory smile. But, past Dr. Kunje's dark head, he saw Ingrid wink at him.

"We're coming down now," Sandy reported suddenly. "The long-range detectors don't indicate any sizable animals in the immediate neighborhood. It's roughly an hour before sunset at this point on the *Macrodiscoi*'s range—is that all right, Dr. Kunje?"

"Yes, that will do very well. The species is mainly diurnal; the night will give us a chance to acclimatize ourselves and become acquainted with the lay of the land before coming into overt contact with other members of the species."

"Very good," Sandy said. "I'll touch down and strip away the shield unit; it'll drift a couple of miles over our heads until we send for it again." A pause, then: "There it goes!"

Abruptly there was a landscape outside, lit by a low afternoon sun; they saw it by way of light-fiber bundles cunningly inserted between the muscles of the stalking-horse that projected their images onto curved screens outside the actual globe. Additionally, of course, they were able to perceive by way of the extensosensors attached to the computer inside the globe, and this Jeff proceeded to do, with an encouraging nod at Dr. Kunje and instructions to close her eyes. A moment to adjust, and then . . .

It was like being the creature as well as himself, seeing the countryside from a height of twenty feet, hearing its noises, smelling its scents, and moreover being aware of the pressure of gravity, the heat of the sun, the multiple and bewildering positions of the limbs carrying the huge, oblate body within which they were hiding. With his own ears he heard Dr. Kunje utter an exclamation; the dry runs they had tried aboard the ship hadn't prepared her for this.

"You'll get used to it," he assured her. "Let's go for a short stroll before nightfall, shall we, Sandy? I think that's a riverbank I can see over to the left. We could try following that, to begin with."

In strict obedience to the computer parasitizing on its nervous system, the artificial *Macrodiscos* plodded on all its many feet in the indicated direction. As they rode along, Jeff confirmed what he had been told about the likeness of this planet to Earth, barring the size of the creatures inhabiting it. Grass, bushes, rocks, the color of the sky, the apparent—not, however, the real—size of the sun, all were astonishingly homelike. When they reached the river and were able to look down at it, they found that it too could have been on Earth: a partly dry, pebble-strewn channel along the bottom of which surged the first water released by the spring thaw in the mountains where it took its rise.

Beside him Jeff heard a mutter which sounded suspiciously like a curse, and glanced around at Dr. Kunje. She had withdrawn from contact with the computer and was shaking her head with a dazed expression. For want of a better idea, Sandy was turning the beast to follow the downstream course of the river.

"Is anything the matter?" Jeff murmured, taking pleasure he was a trifle ashamed of in repeating Dr. Kunje's own words from the moment of his first encounter with the stalking-horse.

"It's—it's confusing at first, that's all," Dr. Kunje said with a glare, and determinedly laid her hands on the contact plates again. "But I think I'm getting the hang of it," she concluded firmly.

"Attagirl," Jeff said under his breath, and added, but not aloud: *You want firsthand data, lady, we provide it for you! Don't blame us when you get exactly what you asked for!*

"Jeff!" Tom Cheliki said suddenly. "Isn't that another of

our own species, over there on the right?"

"Yes!" Couperin, who had been adjusting better than Dr. Kunje to the novel sensation of the contact plate before him, opened his eyes to seek the direct image of the other *Macrodiscos* on the external screens.

"So that's what we look like at the moment!" Tom commented wryly. " 'Tae see oorsel's as ithers see us'— hummm!"

"Not exactly," Dr. Kunje cut in. "That one's a male. You can tell it by the smaller size and generally lighter build, if you look carefully."

It wasn't the first time she had referred to the greater bulk and stature of the female *Macrodiscos*. Jeff repressed the desire to give a thoughtful nod. But it was all fitting together. Something was definitely amiss in Dr. Kunje's view of how to be human, and the more he learned about her, the more he was certain he had pinned down the problem. The cure was going to be both drastic and expensive, but that didn't matter. The *Macrodiscos* would be here next week or next year, awaiting study, but if things were to go on as at present, Dr. Kunje might not be—and people with her degree of brilliance in xenobiology were far and few between.

Seeing that she had closed her eyes and set her mouth in a taut line of concentration, he was able to signal silently to Sandy, whose head tilted at a mischievous angle. Their steed came to a halt.

"Why have you stopped?" Dr. Kunje said, eyes still tightly shut as she fought to absorb and understand the wealth of sensory data furnished by the computer.

"Ought we not to make certain at the first opportunity that other members of the species don't perceive anything wrong with our version of them?" Jeff said.

"Oh—yes, I see. Yes, that's a sensible precaution. Has the male noticed us yet?"

"He surely has," Couperin said. "And what's more, here he comes!"

A quarter-mile distant across the irregular ground, the monster—smaller only by comparison, for he was himself at least forty-eight feet across and fifteen high—had tensed into an alert attitude. All of a sudden, his multiple legs began to propel him violently in their direction.

"That's the aggression reaction!" Dr. Kunje exclaimed. "But what in the . . . ?" Her voice trailed away.

"Aggression reaction?" Sandy repeated. "You mean we ought to get out of here?"

"Well . . ." Dr. Kunje opened her eyes and stared helplessly at the rapidly growing mass of the male as it approached. "Well—yes, I suppose we should."

Compliantly Sandy instructed their steed to move away, but the male wasn't to be shaken off. At a speed between a plod and a gallop, which became a bit uncomfortable after a while because they were having to allow acceleration forces to affect the interior of the globe—there was no choice, short of lifting the entire creature off the ground with their antigravs—they fled across the hillocky plain, sometimes avoiding, sometimes charging straight through the clumps of vegetation that dotted it.

"There's another!" Ingrid said abruptly, and they all noticed that a second male had come into view. Its reaction was identical with the first's: it tensed, hesitated and then charged.

Nobody said anything for a while, as Sandy expertly operated the muscles of their steed. Then a third male appeared and did the same as the others. Sandy contrived to make two of the three collide as they both tried to cut off the same corner around a stand of tall trees, and they forgot the chase in favor of a kind of butting contest, hurling their massive frames at one another with the full force of all their limbs. But the remaining male kept on coming, and inside five minutes there was yet a fourth, discovered as they rounded an outcrop of weathered rocks.

"This isn't precisely what I was led to expect," Jeff said delicately.

"N-no—ah—no, it isn't," Dr. Kunje said with tremendous effort. "Oh, my goodness! There's *another!*" She pointed a shaking hand, and she was quite right. One more male had joined the pursuit, this one smaller than the rest, and correspondingly better able to dodge and twist as he ran.

"Head for the sunset line," Dr. Kunje said in a depressed voice. "As I told you, they're diurnal. Darkness should enable us to—ah—reassess our position."

"It certainly seems to need reassessment," Tom Cheliki said in a tone of disapproval. "I understood that disguised as we are we could venture among these animals without causing any disturbance to their regular activities, instead of which the mere sight of us seems to provoke a clear intention to do us serious mayhem!"

"Look out!" Sandy shouted. Their course had taken them back to the river, at a point where it had cut itself a miniature gorge about forty or fifty feet high, and she had attempted to dodge through the gap. At the same moment one of the pursuing males, displaying improbable powers of reasoning, had scuttled up the bank, and clearly planned to jump down directly on top of them. Only by causing their steed to give a frantic leap was it possible to avoid the impact. The male slammed to the ground in a thrashing tangle of limbs, and a less farsighted member of the posse ran straight into him, provoking the inception of another butting contest.

For a short time thereafter, with the sun slanting closer to the horizon and the sky darkening, they seemed to be on their own again, and from fear of overstressing the muscles she was controlling, Sandy slowed down their headlong run. Shortly, however, one of the males they had left behind reappeared on their trail, moving awkwardly and dragging one of his legs, but determined not to give up; presumably he was the victor of one of the butting contests.

"Here we go again," Sandy said in a resigned tone, and added in a voice that had suddenly changed, "Oh, no! There's a great big patch of woodland ahead of us! We can't just charge straight through it, can we?"

Definitely they could not: enormous or not by Earthly standards, even a full-grown female *Macrodiscos* had to draw the line at trying to brush six-foot tree trunks out of the way like blades of grass.

"So what do we do, Dr. Kunje?" Jeff said in a tone as sweet as honey.

"I . . ." Dr. Kunje put her hand to her head as though dizzy. "I . . ." she said again, and finally, with a miserable cry, managed to finish the sentence.

"I just don't know!"

"Dr. Swann?" Jeff said.

"We could try merely holding off the pursuit until dark," Ingrid said doubtfully. "It's perfectly true that these things prefer to quiet down at nightfall."

"I'll do my best," Sandy promised, and thereafter there followed a kind of weird game of tag as she hurled the colossal mass of their steed back and forth among the fringes of the forest. Twice she managed to crash the blundering male into a tree, so that there was an earth-shaking tremor and a brief respite, but before the determined beast was finally out of the running, one of the others that they had earlier left behind put in an appearance and joined the chase. Then another fresh one showed up, and things went completely out of control. Wherever Sandy headed for, there was one of the animals ahead.

Darkness settled over the land, and contrary to what had been promised, the pursuit did not slacken for a moment. Jeff kept glancing at Dr. Kunje, making it clear that he expected her to say something, and at long last, with face white and lips trembling, she forced it out.

"I'm sorry! Something must have gone wrong—terribly wrong! Perhaps they can sense that this isn't a member of their own species in some way we never guessed at!"

"You mean we should abandon the attempt and make another try on some other occasion?" Jeff suggested.

"I—ah—I can't even see that another try . . ." Dr. Kunje gestured helplessly. "Oh, but the whole thing's absurd! I don't understand! Let's just get out of here!"

"Sandy!" Jeff said quietly, and Sandy, shrugging, prepared to discard the stalking-horse. It's umbrella-like upper frame of bones parted, peeled back, and allowed the landing globe to drift free as the carcass collapsed to the ground. Skillfully she guided the gleaming sphere in among the trees on the fringe of the forest, and at last signaled for the shield unit hovering overhead to come and fetch them back to orbit.

"I don't understand!" Dr. Kunje whispered. "Oh, this is awful! I was so sure it was going to work—we spent months planning this and we double-checked everything. . . . Commander, what can possibly have gone wrong?"

"Stop calling me that," Jeff said in a tone of deliberate crossness. "I don't even allow my own crew to call me that."

"Wh-what?" Dr. Kunje blinked at him, and the brightness in her eyes trickled over and began to course down her cheeks.

Drastic, but essential.

From the corner of his own eye Jeff saw that Ingrid and Couperin were both looking rather embarrassed, as though regretting that they had committed themselves to what they had done. But something of the sort was inescapable; the alternative was for Dr. Kunje to be stretched and broken on the rack of her own need to be infallible.

He said, "What are the males doing now, Tom?"

Tom Cheliki set his hands on the contact plate before him. "Ah . . . sort of snuffing around the empty carcass, as near as I can tell. One of them has drifted off already. It seems to be angry about something. At any rate, it's pulling at trees and bushes as it goes by, trying to uproot them. It looks exactly like someone having a temper tantrum."

"I'm not surprised," Jeff said drily. "Listen, Dr. Kunje! I want you to answer me a couple of questions. First off, how old are you?"

"What in the galaxy has that got to do with—?"

"I asked a question!" Abruptly Jeff's voice was colored with the quality which had made him commander of an Advance Guard crew, a dozen of the most cantankerous, self-willed, and unpredictable species they belonged to. Dr. Kunje's resistance faded into nothing.

"Ah . . . I'm thirty-five. But I don't see why—"

"And at thirty-five, have you ever been in love with anybody? *Have you ever been in love?*"

Indignation flared in her face. "Really, Commander! I don't think you have any right—"

"I said, quit calling me that," Jeff grunted. "All right, I'll take that for a negative. It explains how you could be so stupid as to think you were wrong when in fact you were absolutely, totally, and excessively right."

There was an eternal pause. At last she said weakly, "I was—was *right?*"

"Of course. You're too damned good a biologist not to have been, aren't you? But because you're such a lousy human being—shut up and wait for me to finish!—because you're a lousy human being, you overlooked something that even a complete layman like myself spotted immediately. I'll spell it out for you, since apparently you still haven't caught on."

Jeff drew a deep breath.

"This planet's animal life is pretty close to Earth's, correct? Bisexual, oxygen-breathing, all the rest of it. And as a result of winter-long observations of the *Macrodiscoi,* you had a facsimile prepared of a female of that species that combined all the optimum characteristics you'd noted from your study of them, right? No, you didn't actually say that to me, but I figured it out from your insistence on the larger size of the females. You ordered all the best features of the ones you'd studied combined in this artificial version. True or false?"

"Well, naturally, if we wanted to—" Dr. Kunje began.

"Wait for it! And then, when we actually tried to go out among the *Macrodiscoi* without being observed and a gang of males fell in behind and tried to grab us by the tail, you thought they'd detected the fake and were attacking us, didn't you? Great galaxies, woman, hadn't it occurred to you that this is *spring?*"

He waited for it to sink in. When he had seen the first light of comprehension dawn on her face, he gestured for Sandy to allow the shield unit to settle over the landing globe and carry them away to orbit; she had been holding it off to give him a chance to hit Dr. Kunje with the truth while she was still at her most vulnerable.

"Honestly, Leila!" He used her first name before adding the final clincher, for good psychological reasons. "What do you think would happen if you programmed a computer to simulate an optimum woman? You think you could wander about on Earth without attracting attention? Of course not! Those males who fell in behind and who couldn't be shaken off weren't trying to attack us! All they wanted to do was exactly what you'd expect them to want in the breeding season. They wanted to make love!"

The shield unit halted overhead, and Sandy allowed the globe to drift upwards, clear of the crowns of the nearby trees, and rocket home for the trip back into space.

Leila Kunje put her head in her hands and burst into agonizing sobs.

"Well, I suppose all I can say is thanks very much,"

Ingrid said as she shook Jeff's hand prior to the departure of the Guard ship. But I mean a lot more than just that. I have a feeling that from now on Leila is going to be a hell of a sight more human to work with."

"Don't push her," Sandy said from behind Jeff. "It takes an awfully long time to reintegrate a personality that's wandered as far out of orbit as hers had. But I think you're going to be right in the long run."

"Oh, she has plenty of props," Jeff said. "It isn't everyone in that predicament who's shown what's wrong by being excessively right. That ought to give her a lifeline to follow out of her present depression."

"How long is it going to take to prepare the new male version of the stalking-horse?" Tom Cheliki inquired.

"About a month, I imagine," Couperin said. "By which time the fury of the mating season will be over, and we can conduct our observations under—ah—more relaxed conditions. Are you going to come back and let us borrow one of your landing globes again?"

Jeff grinned and shook his head. "No, I'm afraid our visit was a traumatic experience for Leila. It would be better to call in another Guard ship for the second attempt. In any case, our patrol schedule will take us out of this sector in another couple of weeks. But I'm sure you'll enjoy meeting whoever else is assigned to cover the problem."

There was a pause. Suddenly Ingrid put her arms around him and gave him a smacking kiss on the cheek.

"*That's* more like what I wanted to convey to you," she said with satisfaction. "Working with Leila as she's been most of the time since we joined her here, I'd almost forgotten how to communicate on that level."

"Me, too," Couperin said with enthusiasm, and did the same to Sandy.

"Well, don't forget it again," Jeff said, grinning broadly. "Honestly! Putting down a female on that planet who was the local counterpart of Ninon de l'Enclos, Marilyn Monroe and Anastraea Strange, all rolled into one, and expecting the local males to take no notice—I *ask* you!"

They were still chuckling when the tube linking the Guard ship to the orbital research station parted and the ship went on its lonely way among the stars.

GALACTIC CONSUMER REPORT NO. 2:

AUTOMATIC TWIN-TUBE
WISHING MACHINES

(Extract from Good Buy, *published by
ConGalFedConAss. issue dated July 2329 ESY.)*

Introduction

We have received many letters asking what we think of
twin-tube wishing machines. Typical is the following:

> I'm overworked and underpaid. Sometimes it seems
> there are only two choices left to me—the third,
> suicide, wouldn't help because I can't keep up the
> payments on suicide insurance.
> Either I'll have to have myself twinned so I can
> moonlight a second job—and I don't know what I
> could do that would cover the cost of the twinning—
> or else I'll have to go ten percent deeper into hock
> and buy a wishing machine. At twenty-five thousand
> credits or so they aren't cheap, but on the other
> hand the idea of making everything for ourselves
> seems wonderful. My wife says yes, get one, because
> it would be living like our ancestors used to, com-
> pletely self-sufficient (we have strong pioneer tradi-
> tions here on New Frontier), but I said no, I guess
> there may be a catch, let's wait till *Good Buy* covers
> them.

Not everyone, alas, has that much good sense. Over
the past decade scores of news stories have testified to the
fate of hasty purchasers who succumbed to wild advertising claims.

Swamped by debt, Ebenezer J. Younghusband of Ven-
ables' World boasted to his friends that he'd seen a way

out of his difficulties. He mortgaged his grandchildren's earning capacity to buy a wishing machine. He envisaged making and selling uranium-235 on a rising market to recoup his expenditure. Three thousand casualties occurred, mostly fatal, when he allowed ten kilograms to accumulate in the hopper.

Likewise, rendered desperate by the problem of supporting her eleven children, widowed Mrs. Honoria Quonsett of Hysteria sold six of her offspring to an illegal service agency and invested in a wishing machine, thinking she could redeem them when it had stabilized her affairs. The machine she was able to afford was inadequately insulated against feedback from the user's subconscious, and—since she was naturally concerned with her children's fate above all—began to manufacture duplicates of them. The more frantic she grew, the more the machine churned out. As even the finest machine is unable to create a fully functioning human, ninety-five imbeciles are now a charge on the Hysterian government, and Mrs. Quonsett is permanently hospitalized.

So, if you're considering buying a wishing machine, bear three points in mind: the advertisers' claims are exaggerated; extreme care is always necessary in use; and—most important of all—these machines are *machines,* not magic wands!

Background

Immediately Charlie Voluminous MacDiomnaid, a century or so ago, turned "transmutation without radiation" from a vote-catching slogan into a practical reality, all technically advanced planets began to dream of short-circuiting the conventional manufacturing processes and creating articles at need from crude matter and raw energy.

In 2276 the first notable step toward this goal was accomplished accidentally on Cacohymnia, when Abdul Fidler gave up trying to describe the instruments he wanted to play his famous *Catastrophe Suite* and had himself sliced directly into the computer-operated controls of a woodwind factory. Further development led to one of the two essential elements of a modern manufacturing complex: the visualizer tube, which extracts from the mind of the person in charge the characteristics of the desired product.

The necessity for a second controlling element emerged when Fidler discovered that human musicians couldn't play the instruments he had devised. For his *Variations on the Theme of Planetary Collision* he attempted to surpass his earlier achievement and create a superior musician, too. The life form resulting had an enormous brain, incredibly acute hearing, twenty-eight pairs of hands and sufficient mouths to play eleven wind instruments at once.

On seeing it, Fidler let out a cry of joy approximately a sixth of a tone below G flat in *altissimo*, and the creature—so sensitive it could not endure this deviation from perfect pitch—manipulated him until he was screaming exactly on the note. The loss of his talent was a severe blow to galactic music, but his death established the need for the moderator tube, charged with powers of judgment regarding the feasibility and permissibility of the product. Not unexpectedly, the immense range of the human imagination meant that the early installations had to be huge—the pilot version covered about a hectare of ground.

However, though such size confined the process to commercial undertakings, partial success was better than none, and soon factories working on these principles were a common sight on prosperous planets.

The ultimate target—providing private consumers with home appliances that they need only switch on and think into—appeared as remote as ever until the genius of Gordian Bludgeon, a factoryhand on Odin, broke the deadlock.

One day, during a five-minute period of random thinking intended to clear his mind for a changeover from family spaceboats to sanitary appliances, he snapped his fingers and started to concentrate on the idea of an automatic twin-tube wishing machine no larger than a robochef.

It is pointless to deny that, like so many unsung geniuses, Bludgeon enjoyed imperfect mental stability; however, it is indisputable that without his brilliant inspiration wishing machines for home use would not yet be available. Though refinements have subsequently been incorporated, every machine we found on sale was a modification of his original version.

(Chief among the refinements, incidentally, is the elimination of a circuit he included because his former girlfriend had just married the factory manager. It is now illegal to describe in print what this was intended to do, but by reading between the lines of the distorted account in Harold Knockermaker's *Bludgeon the Man*, any averagely aggressive male should be able to figure it out.)

Brands Tested

We found a total of seven wishing machines that fitted the strict definition of "twin-tube" (i.e., having both a visualizer and a moderator) and "automatic" (i.e., not requiring the preliminary insertion of ready-made parts). All of them cost in the region of twenty-five thousand credits.

Cheaper models are on offer, but they lack the moderator tube. *They should not be bought under any circumstances.* The fact that Eblis is currently quarantined from the rest of the galaxy and languishing under the most savage dictatorship in history is directly attributable to the purchase by a Mrs. Phobia Luncheon of such a machine. Her five-year-old son, Elgin, in a tantrum over the refusal of an ice-cream soda, started the machine and set it to making nuclear-armed robot soldiers two meters tall, with whose aid he overran the planet and set up a drugstore with a soda fountain a kilometer long. (He is expected to die of malnutrition in about 2335, but it is impossible to estimate how many of Eblis's population will survive him.)

These are the models we tested, and the chief slogans used to advertise them:

Cornucopia: "A Horn of Plenty in the Home"
Midas: "Better than the Golden Touch"
Croesus: "Everything money can or can't buy"
Inexhaustible: "Everyone is on the make!"
Zillionaire: "Beyond the dreams of avarice"
Wizard: "Magical manufacturing"
Domesticated Djinn: "There is no God but Allah; however, the profit is entirely yours"

On inspection, the *Midas* and *Croesus,* proved to be

identical except for the nameplate affixed in the front of the cabinet. The former costs two hundred credits more than the latter. The makers refused to comment on this.

Appearance and Finish

With the following qualifications the finish of the products was rated "acceptable" by our test panel.

The *Cornucopia* is nearly twice as big as the largest of the others, and the makers recommend that the first use it be put to after purchase is the construction of an extra room to hold it.

The output hopper supplied with the *Midas* and *Croesus* imposes an arbitrary limit on the size of articles manufactured. Anything larger than approximately two by three meters comes out concertinaed. In the end we sent for one of the range of nonstandard oversize hoppers available at extra charge. (We tried making our own with the machine, but the tolerances were of the order of two micrometers and the controls were insufficiently precise.)

The *Domesticated Djinn* is inscribed all over with excerpts from the Koran and is time-switched to prevent its use when the owner was supposed to be facing Mecca for prayer. Five periods of nonavailability per day, each lasting fifteen minutes, may constitute a drawback in the view of non-Moslems.

The *Zillionaire* is smaller than the others in every respect, including its visualizer cap, which fitted only one of our test panel (an eight-year-old boy chosen for the vividness of his imagination). We had to substitute the cap from the basically similar *Wizard*. The user's chair was rated "very uncomfortable" by the entire panel, and we had to pack it with foam padding before anyone could sit through a production cycle.

The *Inexhaustible* posed us several problems. Our attention had already been caught by the curious advertising copy announcing it. (Sample: "MOST SPLENDIFEROUS THE NOT COSTLY WISHING MACHINE. YOU WANT, IT MAKE, NO MATTER WHATEVER THE DESIRE WITHIN REASONS OF COARSE!")

The attractive gray cabinet is finished in a manner we had not previously encountered. When touched, it humps and rubs against the hand, at the same time secreting a gummy fluid with a strong smell resembling banana oil. The output (no hopper is fitted) is on top of the casing and can only be reached by stepladder. The controls are on two boards at opposite ends of the housing, which means that unless the user's reach exceeds 3.2 meters and he has had the foresight to install wall mirrors to reflect the dials, he has to walk back and forth all the time. This is rendered difficult by the hard, flat bench, tilted at thirty-five degrees, fitted in place of a user's chair. Also, there is no visualizer cap; twenty-one separate leads have to be attached to the head with suction cups, and the handbook advises shaving before use.

Instruction Manuals, etc.

Handbooks are supplied with five of the machines. That for the *Cornucopia* promises: "No adjustment will be required for at least one Earth Standard Year." (But see below, *Performance.*) The cheaper *Croesus* has a handbook; the *Midas* does not, which seems odd. We used the same for both. That for the *Domesticated Djinn* opens with an invocation: "In the name of Allah, the Merciful, let no harm befall users of this machine!" (Again, see below.)

The *Zillionaire* has no instructions except a swing-ticket attached to the on-off switch, which reads: "Any fault that develops in this machine can easily be rectified by having it produce a replacement part." We should like to repeat the comment of our eight-year-old, but this publication has to go through the Galactic mails.

The instructions for the *Wizard* are in 174 languages, an admirable idea. Unfortunately the text in 173 of them (the exception being High Canal Martian) refers to an earlier model discontinued four years ago.

The manual for the *Inexhaustible* has apparently been produced on the machine by an inexperienced operator. It is a handsome volume of about a hundred pages, of which all but the first sixteen are blank.

Guarantees

The guarantee for the *Cornucopia* is acceptable, subject
to the deletion (don't forget to thumbprint it in the margin)
of the clause which runs: "The manufacturers will not be
held liable for (*a*) the products of a diseased imagination;
(*b*) operation of the machine by a minor; (*c*) death,
disablement, or disfigurements of any user by his/her
productions."

None of the other guarantees is worth the permafilm
they are printed on. The *Domesticated Djinn's* states, *inter
alia*, "Omission of five-times-daily prayer voids this warranty." The *Zillionaire's* says: "We reserve the right to
cancel this or any other ostensible warranty at our entire
discretion." The *Inexhaustible's* has at least the virtue of
honesty (we think); it runs simply: "We decline responsi-
bilities, all shapes, all sizes, all colors."

Power Source and Mode of Operation

As stated above, all wishing machines on sale are similar
to Bludgeon's original concept. The user sits in a chair
(*Inexhaustible:* scrambles back and forth over a sloping
bench) and puts on a cap connected to the visualizer (*Inexhaustible:* shaves scalp and attaches twenty-one leads),
adjusts manual controls to broad categories of mass,
switches on the power and concentrates on visualizing the
appearance and performance of a known end product, or
the performance of something desired but not hitherto
invented. This eventually appears in the output hopper,
or not, as the case may be.

The *Midas, Croesus* and *Wizard* are fitted with a useful
extra: a warning bell on the moderator to indicate if production of the article has been vetoed. With the slower
machines, especially the *Zillionaire*, it is sometimes possible
to hang around hopefully for an hour or more before
realizing that nothing is going to emerge.

The *Cornucopia, Midas/Croesus* and *Wizard* draw
domestic current on planets where a piped-plasma grid
exists; otherwise they require a portable fusion plant. The

Domesticated Djinn and *Zillionaire* can also be run off solar or other energy sources, but performance on anything but plasma is unsatisfactory. The *Zillionaire,* using solar energy, required six and a half hours of steady concentration to produce a meal for two people, which the hungry tester then immediately devoured.

The *Inexhaustible* is unique in having to be primed with twelve kilograms of technetium (this is apparently what the advertisements mean by "SELF-CONTAINING SAUCE OF POWER—OUTSIDE POWER IS NEEDLES! ! !"). The cost of furnishing this initial load is about seventeen thousand credits; however, an efficient auxiliary circuit keeps the level of fuel constant, using thermal energy from the air of the room, providing sufficient downtime is allowed.

Performance

Theoretically a wishing machine will make almost anything, subject to the veto of the moderating tube. In practice, the latter is by no means consistent, and what you get out depends anyhow on how good you are at concentrating. (It also depends on how good the visualizer tube is at sifting conscious from subconscious mental images.)

It was clearly impossible to attempt a cross section of users' desires. We settled for three groups of tests.

First, we had to establish that everyday requirements could be met. We instructed the testers to make (*a*) a meal for two people which they personally enjoyed; (*b*) clothing for themselves, from hat to shoes; (*c*) an item of household equipment, preferably furniture.

All passed, with the following qualifications:

Food produced on the initial runs of the *Cornucopia* resisted knives, forks and teeth, and its piece of furniture (a table) proved to be of collapsed steel. We had to send for a crane to remove it from the output hopper. Investigation showed that the durability control needed adjustment; it was set to "101 percent." A setting of one produced edible food and twenty-five produced usable furniture in later runs.

Clothing manufactured on the *Midas* was adequately

warm and waterproof, but when we sent out a female tester in the garments she had made, to see how well they wore, the next we heard of her she was in jail on a charge of indecent exposure. Hers, and all other female clothing produced by this machine, turned perfectly transparent one hour after putting on. A complaint to the makers produced an apology and a statement to the effect that the factory-hand in charge of this batch has been sent for psychotherapy to eliminate his Peeping-Tom syndrome.

All the testers who ate meals prepared by the *Domesticated Djinn* were hospitalized with acute food poisoning.

The *Inexhaustible* needed enormous extra effort before it would produce food uncontaminated with bromine and arsenic and of any other color than purple (though some of our testers found purple steak and potatoes attractive visually, they tasted bad), or clothing less than four centimeters in thickness, devoid of fiberglass scales and with sleeves less that 1.8 meter long.

Second, we had to establish that it was economical to produce household durables available through more conventional channels. We tried for a threevee set and an air conditioner.

In all cases it was cheaper (sometimes one hundred percent cheaper) to buy commercially. However, the following points should be noted:

The *Cornucopia*, in response to a tester who claimed not to have the faintest notion of how a threevee set works, produced one in working order, superior to any we had ever seen and based on what proved to be a radical new means of receiving broadcast signals. We are working on this and hope shortly to market a commercial version, which may go some way toward making up the anticipated deficit in next year's balance sheet. (See "Message from your Chairman," this issue.)

Sets made by the *Zillionaire* would not receive anything, but merely repeated what the tester was visualizing at the time. We had to fire one tester whose set depicted a positively obscene episode from *Peyton Planet*. And those from the *Domesticated Djinn* would receive only Mecca, Medina, and New Cairo.

The air conditioners mostly worked okay, except for

the *Inexhaustible*'s. After a few minutes' operation, the room was full of the reek of chlorine, and inspection showed that a miniature transmuter had been set into the housing, which was busy getting rid of the oxygen in favor of chlorine, bromine, iodine, and inert gases.

Finally we had to determine how safe the machines are. There is no Galactic Standard yet, but an Earthside law lays down that the moderator must prevent the creation of "any noxious or vicious article, object, or creature whatsoever." Cutouts built into the moderator are supposed to enforce this.

In practice, it's clear that definitions vary. Even on the best of the machines, the *Cornucopia*, all testers were able to make infectious bacteria (see *Obituary*, inside back cover). And our eight-year-old, using the *Zillionaire*, was able to make a spanking machine (from which his parents were rescued in a state of extreme exhaustion), a suit of battle armor, his own size, in which to make good his escape, and enough sleepy-gas to blank out the ConGalFed-ConAss Building while he was leaving.

We will not go into detail on the tests we conducted for adult fantasy, except to point out that on all planets with stringent blue laws importation of the *Domesticated Djinn* is forbidden. It is specifically designed to make mindless but beautiful houris, and two divorces are pending among our panel of testers.

Our performance tests of the *Inexhaustible* were inconclusive. We were tempted to abandon them when we discovered that, although insulation against subconscious feedback leaves something to be desired on all the machines, the insulation on this one tends to filter out conscious images and let subconscious ones go through. (The events which led us to this impression need to be gone into, as the tests were abortive.)

However, we felt we owed it to our members to determine whether the extravagant claim implied in the trade name *Inexhaustible* is true or false. Our change of address, noted on the inside cover, stems largely from our persistence.

We decided to make up a cyclic tape for some article of which any family is likely to consume large quantities, and run it until the machine stopped working. Our first choice was paper handkerchiefs, but the machine's vulnerability to subconscious associations compelled the Greater New York Public Health Authority to step in. (We were glad to learn, just before press time, that the influenza epidemic is officially "under control.")

It was then suggested that the item which a family consumes most is *money*.

This choice had the secondary advantage that the use of a wishing machine to make galactic currency is counterfeiting, and if the machine's moderator permitted an illegal act, we would be compelled to inform our members that it was an offense to buy one.

We regret to announce that on this test the machine performed flawlessly. Our calculations show that the technetium will run out when the pile of bills now covering the site of our former headquarters is about three hundred twenty meters high, unless a strong wind gets up, so the machine is not in fact "inexhaustible," but this is a slim consolation. (Anyone finding wind-blown bills, incidentally, is requested to forward them to the office of our Attorney for the Defense before the first of next month, when the case is due for hearing.)

Value for Credits

The *Cornucopia* performs reasonably well, and its guarantee can be rendered acceptable by one deletion. Although it is capable of considerable improvement, we are bound to name it as our Best Buy.

Not Recommended

We learn from the Superdistrict Attorney's staff that an investigation has been made into the origins of the *Inexhaustible*. It emanates from a space-going factory parked about a thousand parsecs outside the galaxy in the direction of Andromeda. The authorities are proceeding on the assumption that it represents an economic assault by the dominant civilization of M-31. The design of it accords with the known characteristics of that race: they would be very comfortable on the sloping bench provided for the user, they have arms and eyes at both ends of their bodies and are extremely tall, so would be able to operate the divided controls as well as to fish the end product out of the top, and they prefer an atmosphere of chlorine, iodine, neon, and argon.

Do not—repeat, *do not*—buy this machine! Apart from its being capable of an illegal act (counterfeiting), our advice is that it can only be properly controlled by an Andromedan. If you meet anyone who claims to have had no trouble with an *Inexhaustible,* report him at once to the nearest office of the Galactic Bureau of Investigation. He's probably an Andromedan spy.

DEATH DO US PART

They had just declared an official drought, which meant that for the past fifteen days less than some infinitesimal quantity of rain had fallen over southern England. But it was a good deal worse than an ordinary drought. Since it began, the sky had been a leaden, cloudless blue, and the sun had glowered like a bloodshot eye on the streets of London, turning gardens to tinder and nerves to rags. Its setting brought no relief; by their millions the sleepless populace sweltered and fretted in their beds.

It was going to be like that again tonight, Arthur Jordan reflected as he let himself into his apartment overlooking Hampstead Heath. Wiping palms sticky from the handle of his attaché case, he flung wide all the windows.

The air in the room, which had been tightly closed since he departed for the office that morning, was like an oven. The air outside was like a furnace. Even the breeze which now and again stirred the listless leaves of the trees on the heath brought no hint of coolness.

Arthur Jordan groaned. His mind filled with wild plans to circulate ice water through the central heating system, but, of course, it wouldn't work if these reports in the evening papers about a water famine were correct—which brought him to the realization that he might as well enjoy a cold tub while he had the chance.

He peeled off his sweat-damp clothes as he walked across the living room and recklessly turned on the tap.

The water turned warm even as he sat in it, and when he stepped out, the thirsty air dried him almost before he could reach a towel. Despairingly he went as he was into the kitchen to collect ice cubes from the overworked refrigerator and mix something to heal his parched throat.

He came back with a glass tall and cool in his hand,

and there was someone standing in the middle of the living room.

Arthur dropped the glass with a crash, and the stranger swung around. The expression on his face changed through varying shades of polite apology, astonishment and embarrassment—and he vanished.

Weakly, Arthur clung to the back of the nearest chair. His bare foot fell on an ice cube in the puddle left by the spilled drink, and he came to himself with a start.

There was no one else in the room. There couldn't be. He had locked the door behind him when he came in, and the windows overlooking the heath were thirty feet above ground; an insect might get in that way, but not a man.

For a few seconds he held his head between sweating hands. Then he went determinedly back into the kitchen and mixed a fresh drink. He swallowed it before harm could come to it, and set the glass down empty.

"It's the heat," he assured himself aloud. "Maybe I have a touch of sunstroke."

He wasn't completely convinced, but when he looked through the living-room door again, there was no sign of the intruder. He picked up a dustpan and brush for the broken glass and a cloth with which to wipe the carpet, and went to clean up the mess.

He was bending to the task when a polite cough sounded behind him, and a diffident voice spoke.

"Your pardon, sir! Are you by good chance Mr. Arthur Jordan, the lawyer?"

Arthur lost his balance and almost fell on the splintered glass, only catching himself at the last moment. Trying frantically to turn the damp cloth into a kind of kilt, he spun around.

There *was* someone in the room. A man. A short, quite youthful man with a snub nose, who wore—in the middle of a raging heat wave!—knee breeches and a long coat and a powdered wig, a tricorn hat in his hand, and a sword slung low at his side.

And everything about him from his face to his buckled shoes was a darker or lighter shade of silvery gray, as though a badly exposed photograph had come to life.

"I beg your pardon heartily indeed for intruding upon you when you are—ahem!—thus unprepared for visitors, sir," the intruder continued. There was a hint of north country accent in his voice. "But, believe me, it is—ah—quite imperative!"

For a few moments Arthur struggled to impose order on the boiling currents in his mind. He failed, and let go the single question that was all he could manage after the shock.

"How did you get in here?" he blared.

The other shifted from foot to foot, trying to avoid Arthur's searing gaze. "My deepest apologies, sir!" he exclaimed.

"I don't care how deep they are!" roared Arthur. "What do you mean by breaking in and daring to stand there while I—while I—"

The improvised kilt proved a failure at that point, and he dodged behind the back of the chair on which he had tossed his trousers on the way to the bathroom. A man without trousers, he reasoned, was at a disadvantage under any circumstances, and if he did have to cope with an intruder who seemed to have got lost from a fancy-dress ball, he saw no point in handicapping himself unnecessarily.

"The truth of the matter is," said the stranger, fidgeting with some braid on his sword belt. "The truth is, sir—" The words came with a rush and a sudden lapse into broad Yorkshire. "I'm a bogle!"

The trousers secured, Arthur came cautiously forward, trying to estimate how long he would need to reach the phone and call the police. "Won't you sit down?" he said soothingly. "This heat is enough to try anyone, I'm sure."

"Sir, I thank you," said the stranger, placing his hat on a nearby table. "But in my present state I do not feel the need to—ahem!—relieve my limbs of their burden."

"You mean you're not staying?" hazarded Arthur feebly.

"No, sir. With your leave, I do propose to remain so long as is needful—oh, but I perceive you are not familiar with the northern word I used in the haste of the moment!" He drew himself up to his full height.

"I, sire, am what you would call a spirit, or specter. In the verna-*cu*lar"—his stress was wrong—"I am a spook."

"Yes, yes," muttered Arthur, deciding that perhaps it would be better to make for the door than the phone.

"If you doubt my word——" the stranger began, laying his hand on his sword, then checking himself with a rueful grin. "I forget myself. 'Tis not the fashion these days, I do believe, to settle slights by the rapier. I'faith, I would not myself lightly have credited such a tale. In earnest of my truthfulness, then, allow me——"

He vanished again.

Arthur felt as though his head would burst. He stared around the room. There, forgotten on the table, was the tricorn hat. He put his hand out to it, gingerly. It was solid to the touch, but when he picked it up, he found it weighed literally nothing; it felt, in fact, as though it wasn't there.

His heart pounding, he stepped to the place where the self-styled ghost had been, and walked through what was now indisputably empty air.

"Have I persuaded you, sir?" the voice inquired from behind him.

Arthur put the hat back on the table. He nodded weakly and dropped into a chair.

The ghost came forward and reclaimed his headgear. With a flourish, he bowed to his unwilling host.

"Allow me to present myself, sir. James Shaw of Clayhurst"—he caught himself, again with that rueful smile—"late of Clayhurst, in the county of Yorkshire, at your service." He sat down on a hard chair facing Arthur, spreading his coattails to right and left.

"Now, sir, I am correct, am I not, in believing you a lawyer?"

"Y-yes," Arthur admitted.

"Then I have grave need of your services. Though how I shall pay your fee I know not, sin' my worldly goods were despoiled . . ."

"Don't let that worry you," interrupted Arthur. "After all, it's quite an honor in itself to be consulted by a"—he swallowed painfully—"ghost."

"Sir, I am truly indebted for your kindness. Well, to the heart of it. I wish to have—ahem!—my marriage dissolved. What, in the parlance of your day, is termed a 'divorce'."

"*What?*"

"A divorce." Shaw seemed to be gaining confidence. "I

heard from sundry shades who shared my plight tempo-
rarily during the late terrible war fought betwixt this
country and the Germanies that such separation may be
more easily come by than in my day—though surely," he
added, sighing, "if ever an age would give relief to marriage, mine should have, that held the bond so cheap."

"But how"—Arthur's voice refused point-blank to come
under proper control—"how can a ghost have a divorce?"

"That, sir," said Shaw, with a shake of his head, "is the
point on which I crave your aid."

Arthur passed a hand across his forehead. "I'm afraid
you've picked on the wrong person," he said. "I'm an
expert in company law, specializing in matters of trade, or
business. I've never done any divorce work."

For a moment Shaw looked so crestfallen that Arthur
felt a twinge of pity. He added, "But I'll do what I can, of
course!"

"Sir, I shall be eternally grateful," asserted the ghost
with relief. "And mark you, being as I am—alas!—an
immortal creature, that is not lightly said."

"But before we go any further—" Arthur got up and
made for the kitchen. He came back with the bottle of
whiskey he had been drawing on when Shaw had showed
up, his remaining stock of ice, and—after some hesitation—two glasses.

"Ah . . . I don't know whether . . . ?" he ventured,
indicating the second glass.

"Nor I, sir!" said Shaw, perking up considerably. "But
I've no wish to delay finding out!"

He drank with enthusiasm. Arthur tore his mind away
from the fascinating problem of what a ghost could do
with something as material as whiskey, gulped his own
drink and resumed his chair.

"I think you'd better give me a few more details," he
suggested.

"Know then, sir," said the ghost, wiping his lips with
an enormous and beautiful kerchief of the same silvery
gray as the rest of him, "that I was—am—was the son of
a wool merchant of Yorkshire, and grew up there at
Clayhurst Hall. Though my father was but a rough man,
he had amassed much wealth and saw to it that I received
a gentleman's education. To my sorrow, however, when I

was but twenty years of age, my father died, and my mother did not long outlast him.

"I, though, was a lively youth, and—ahem!—personable, and did seek to improve myself in the company of my betters. I therefore left my inheritance in the charge of my father's bailiff and lived much of the year in London. In that road I prospered. I was well acquainted with my lord Greenhough, and my lady Gosport, and Sir Charles Tregarron . . ."

Watching, Arthur saw the faint swell of pride that accompanied this recital of the names of the forgotten great. He could clearly picture how it had been: a lonely, country-bred boy striving to keep up with the bucks and Corinthians of a rakehell age. He began to be really interested.

For a few moments Shaw fell silent, thinking of a departed day. Then he coughed and resumed.

"But when I was six-and-twenty years of age," he went on, "I bethought me I should take a wife and settle down. If truth be told—ahem!—my patrimony was wasted somewhat. Then I fell in love.

"I could have—you will pardon me speaking thus ignobly of a lady, sir, but this is betwixt man and man—I could have enjoyed her charms without the rites of matrimony. But no, poor fool that I was: needs must I marry her and carry her off in triumph to my boyhood home. Kitty Tregarron it was, the niece of Sir Charles—which weighed more than it should have done with me. I thought overmuch of a connection with that family. . . .

"Ahem! After our wedding we began the long journey northward. You will understand me when I say that I had quite turned Kitty's head, so that we were impatient, and paid but little attention to the country about.

"While we were yet but a few miles from London, crossing Hampstead Heath—we were to reach our first post quite shortly, and it was full dark—we were set upon by highwaymen. Though my coachman, brave lad, discharged his pistol at the thieves, they overpowered us. In terror lest they be discovered, they . . ."

"They—ahem!" That nervous cough was catching! "They killed you?" ventured Arthur.

Shaw nodded, his head bent. "Alas, yes! They dragged

us thence to a grave on the bare heathland, which no man ever found."

"And you became ghosts?"

"In sooth," Shaw answered bravely. "Myself, and my wife, Kitty, too."

"And the coachman?"

Shaw shook his head. Forestalling Arthur's next question, he said, "I cannot say why, sir. There are laws, it would appear. But there are no lawyers to expound them to us."

Arthur let the point pass. He said, "Go on."

"At first I bore it with considerable fortitude. But then, alas, my sweet wife Kitty, who in the fashionable whirl of London and Bath had been so airy and genteel, proved on lasting acquaintance to be nothing more than a nagging shrew. A very nagging shrew!" He lingered over the words, and then turned beseechingly to Arthur.

"Sir, may you never know what it is to be the sole company of a sharp-tongued woman for nigh on two hundred year!"

Arthur shivered. The ghost had something there, no denying!

"Why haven't you done something about it before now?" he demanded. "Two hundred years is an unconscionable time to wait."

Shaw agreed sadly. "T'faith, it is. But it was not till some few years ago—I know not how long—that I began to devise a plan. In my day it was a weary business to undo the bonds of matrimony, and consequently it was the habit to ignore them when they proved irksome. The possibility never occurred to me that I might inquire for a divorce."

"Haven't you at least tried to get away from your wife?"

"Often and often—though less so in recent times. We speak but little these past fifty years. Still, between sunset and cockcrow we may walk, so I have passed time in trying to escape. But I encountered—ahem!—a difficulty. Know you that a spirit such as I is bounden not to cross a running stream?"

Arthur sat up with a jerk. "Of course! The drains! The sewers!"

"You hit it exactly. I have ever been turned aside by the water beneath the earth—until this blessed drought which is upon us."

Arthur put his head back and laughed loudly and long. Shaw sat with a hurt look, staring at the wall.

"I'm sorry," Arthur choked, wiping tears of mirth from his eyes. "I wasn't laughing at your predicament, I swear. It just seemed so funny that, while everyone else in London is cursing the heat wave, you're glad of it. Have another drink?"

Shaw hesitated. "You are too kind, sir. But—have you by chance a drop of clarry about the house?"

"I'm afraid not," Arthur admitted.

"Ah, sometimes I crave a sip of such clarry as my lady Gosport kept—shame on me, I'm an ingrate! Pour, sir; your liquor is a comfort to my heart."

When the glasses were full again, Arthur went on, "I'm the one who should be grateful to you, you know. I think this is the only really interesting case I've ever been given. The trouble is, I don't see what can possibly be done for you. There's no legal precedent for divorcing a dead man."

"A—spirit—I spoke with in the late war," Shaw said tentatively, "spoke of a man missing for seven years and declared dead, upon whose return the decree was set aside. Since the law takes no cognizance of ghosts, I wondered whether I might make an appearance . . ."

"Hmmm!" Arthur rubbed his chin. "No, I'm afraid not. After going on two hundred years, they're not going to set aside a legal presumption of death, even though you told me your grave was never found. And in any case you say you can walk only between—uh—sunset and cock-crow. Courts only sit during the day, for one thing. Besides, there must be scores of drains and watermains between here and anywhere a court could hear your application. No, it doesn't look hopeful," he finished with genuine regret. The idea of confronting his dustier colleagues in the department of probate, admiralty and divorce with a suit by a ghost greatly appealed to him.

Shaw said with emphasis, "The devil take all legal quiddities!" His face set, he rose and bowed. "I apologize for wasting your time, then, sir!"

"No, don't go." Arthur jumped up and thrust him back

on his chair. The sensation was the same as the one he had felt when he picked up the hat; there was solidity, but absolutely no mass behind it. "I think you're one of the most interesting people I've ever met, and I'm not going to turn you out to wander on the heath in this weather. And you never know—if I think the problem over for a while, I may come up with an idea."

"I'm obleeged to you, sir," Shaw said with relief. "It will indeed be a pleasure to have genteel company after so long."

In the clear light of morning—which was far from cold, for the temperature at dawn was well into the sixties— Arthur rubbed his aching head and looked around him. He had had a dream of the wildest kind. It must be due to heatstroke. He sat up and saw a playing card on the floor just inside the bedroom door.

Of course: he'd been teaching James to play canasta, and the ghost had sworn it would have been the rage of Bath in his day. . . .

James?

The *ghost?*

With a groan, Arthur climbed off the bed and went into the living room. On the table in the middle: two glasses, one empty bottle of whiskey, one bowl with a little water in the bottom which had once held ice cubes, the cards, an ashtray half-full of butts. . . .

He drew a deep breath. No dream, that. He really had sat here with James Shaw, late of Clayhurst in Yorkshire. He really had gotten on first-name terms. He really had heard scandalous stories of the eighteenth-century nobility that had never reached the history books. (That had been rather fun.)

Which meant that in all probability that he really had finished up by shouting an invitation to the fading specter to come back and haunt him whenever he liked.

He ran for the bathroom and soaked his head in cold water to help himself adjust to the idea. Little by little he did so; in fact, his mind kept straying all morning from the intricacies of the case of breach of contract supposed to be engaging his attention to the absurd but intriguing problems of arranging a divorce for a ghost. He made no progress at all, but he enjoyed himself tremendously; more than once the firm's gaunt and solemn head clerk eyed him reprovingly because he had let slip a chuckle.

On his way back from lunch he stopped at his wine merchant and bought a bottle of whiskey to replace the one emptied last night. To this purchase he added, on impulse, a bottle of the firm's finest claret for James's benefit.

Then the blow fell. The head clerk greeted him on his return to the office with the news that one of the senior partners had been taken ill; the doctor had diagnosed heat prostration and ordered complete rest, and Arthur would have to stand in for him at dinner this evening with a very important client.

Some time last night he had acquired a collection of eighteenth-century expletives, far more mouth-filling than their pallid modern counterparts. He astonished the clerk with a pyrotechnic display of them, and then resigned himself wearily to looking after the client. He left the office early to dash home and set out the bottle of claret on the table for James, together with a note addressed to "James Shaw Esquire" explaining what had happened, and headed back into the hot maw of the West End to meet the fly in the ointment and take him to dinner.

Ezra Maxton, formerly of Carchemish, New Jersey, was a great deal more like an English preconception of an American than Arthur would have believed possible. He put the fact down to some sort of protective coloration. The matter on which he had consulted Arthur's firm was complex, involving the transfer of assets and the creation of a subsidiary company in London; there were patent rights and tax problems and contracts to be seen to. In the normal course of events Arthur would have reckoned to straighten out the basics in an hour's hard talking and go ahead from there.

Unfortunately, not only was he himself in a distracted mood—partly due to James, partly to the heat—but Ezra Maxton was apparently a much-married man, intent on turning the business discussion with dinner into an evening on the town. Arthur gave up all hope of getting back to see James at a reasonable hour, and wearily consented to go on after dinner to a nightclub. He had drunk rather a lot with dinner. It was hot in the club, and he drank more. His grip on his surroundings slipped steadily.

Maxton, by contrast, expanded as fast as the carnation in his lapel wilted. At midnight he was giving Arthur a lecture, illustrated with color photos, on his family unto the third and fourth generations; by half-past he was enthusiastically telling a bowl of flowers about English tradition and the quaintness of London.

Then Arthur caught the tail end of a sentence and sat up with a start.

"What was that about a ghost?" he demanded, trying to fix Maxton with a glare—the American kept wandering about.

"Huh?" Maxton blinked. "I was just saying that we found the greatest little house in Hampstead to live in while we're over here. It's been modernized, sure, but outside it's like it was hundreds of years ago. The only thing it doesn't have is a ghost."

"Do you want a ghost?" said Arthur, his heart pounding.

"Why—I guess it would be appropriate," Maxton agreed, grinning to show he went along with the gag. "Mind you, not the kind that goes around rattling chains and raising Cains—Cain. No, just a high-class specter to add tone to the joint."

"I can get you one," said Arthur owlishly. He had just seen the way out of James's predicament.

"You're a great kidder!" exclaimed Maxton. "Here, have another drink."

"I'm serious," Arthur insisted. "I can get you a ghost. Guaranteed quiet and respectable. And he's awfully high-class—in fact, when he was alive, he was the nephew-in-law of a baronet!"

"That sounds fine," soothed Maxton. "Now have this drink I poured for you."

"No," said Arthur, getting to his feet. "You said you wanted a ghost, I can get you one. Law of shupply—supply and demand. Come on."

He dragged the bewildered American into a taxi, praying—as soon as he realized what he had done—that James had been too tempted by the bottle of claret to leave the apartment yet. He could imagine himself getting into all kinds of embarrassing trouble if he went out over Hampstead Heath in the middle of the night shouting for a man who'd been dead for two centuries.

But James was there, sitting over a half-empty glass and crying—intangible tears of ectoplasm, presumably.

He brightened on seeing Arthur and jumped to his feet. At Arthur's whispered order to make himself invisible, he looked pained, but he caught on when he saw Maxton in the doorway.

It was presumably the claret that made his vanishing a slower and more piecemeal process than usual; for quite ten seconds after Maxton came in, there was a ghostly ruffle visible against the bathroom door. Fortunately, the visitor didn't notice it.

Arthur sat Maxton down in a chair as a precaution, hoped his heart was in good condition, and poured the last of the claret into three glasses including James's. Then he spoke to the air.

"James? Will you come back now?"

There was a pause, during which he found himself utterly convinced the whole affair was impossible and he would have to pass his behavior off as a practical joke . . . and there was James.

"Good day to the both of you!" the ghost exclaimed. Maxton swung to where the voice had originated, and nearly fell off his chair.

"That's a great trick!" he said warmly. "How does it work?"

Arthur ignored the question. He said, "Allow me to present to you the—uh—the late Mr. James Shaw of Clayhurst, Yorkshire." He swallowed hard. "James, this is Ezra Maxton. He's from America."

"Ah, a colonial!" James said. "I'm honored, sir," he added with a wobbly bow.

"Mr. Maxton has taken a lease on a house near here," Arthur explained. "He wants a ghost to go with it. Would you care to oblige—I mean, obleege him?"

"You've found a way to break this tie that binds me to my Kitty?" the ghost asked, half-fearfully.

"I think so," confirmed Arthur, and drew a deep breath. "Tell me, were you married according to the rites of the Church of England?"

"Of course! Think you I'm a Papist?"

"Thank goodness," muttered Arthur. He found he had crossed his fingers unconsciously; uncrossing them, he went on, "Now, listen. Marriage is binding as a civil contract, but it has—like all my favorite contracts—an escape clause. I make my living by spotting them.

"Do you remember the bit about 'till death do us part'?"

For a moment James looked blank. Then he gave a shout of joy and broke into a wild country dance, waving his hat.

"Arthur, I'm forever in your debt! You mean I'm not tied to my Kitty after all!"

Arthur beamed fatuously. "That's right. You agreed to have and to hold until—etcetera. And you are dead. So you can leave her any time you like."

He glanced at Maxton, who was clutching his glass—empty—in white-knuckled hands. "Won't keep you a moment, Mr. Maxton," he apologized, and turned back to James.

"You haven't made any subsequent undertaking to stay where you—uh—live?"

James shook his head. "I told you: time and time again I've essayed to depart from there, and all that held me back was this cursed running water beneath the ground."

"We'll solve that problem when we come to it. Hold on while I get some paper and I'll draw you up a contract that *is* foolproof." Singing a bawdy ballad James had taught him the night before, he went to rummage through his desk.

It was probably the strangest legal document ever concocted, but it was solid as a rock—Arthur was certain of that. It bound the ghost of James Shaw, Esq., late—etcetera —to haunt the premises of "Gables," Mecklingen Road, Hampstead, leased by the undersigned Ezra Maxton, formerly of Carchemish, New Jersey, for the duration of his supernatural existence or until the demolition of the house, with options to extend or terminate the tenancy as subsequently agreed. In return, James Shaw was accorded the sole right of ghostly occupancy.

"You see," Arthur pointed out happily as he wrote in a

signature block, "if you have the sole rights, Kitty won't be able to come bothering you. You can change your mind if you so decide, but you'll have to get me or someone else to alter the contract. Now sign here."

The ghost seized the pen and wrote his name excitedly. Arthur witnessed the signature and turned to Maxton. "Now if you'll just—Good Lord, he's asleep! Well, he asked for a ghost and ghost he shall have. Help me wake him up."

It took some doing, but eventually Maxton's shaky signature was on the contract alongside James's. Arthur blotted it and folded the document neatly. He slipped it into a drawer of his desk and turned the key in the lock.

"If Kitty tries to make trouble for you, James, just refer her to me," he said. "I'll see to it. And now what we have to do is get you to your new home."

He phoned for a taxi and they set out for Maxton's place. The cabby was convinced his passengers were crazy, because they kept making him stop and try alternative routes whenever James felt the queasy sensation by which he recognized running water ahead. More than once Arthur wondered if they would ever find a usable route, but they had picked a good time to try—most people were in bed and consequently water that would have been running if taps had been turned on was standing in the pipes and James could get over it. They succeeded at last.

Maxton let them in his front door. From somewhere upstairs came a soprano shout.

"That you, Ezra honey?"

Maxton groaned softly and bade his companions good night. With a final, apprehensive glance at James, he made for the stairs. By the time he reached the first landing, he was chuckling, and before he disappeared, he was laughing uproariously.

Arthur smiled and closed the front door.

"Well, good luck, James," he said. "Maxton seems like a nice guy, and I'm sure you'll get on with him."

"Sir—" James seemed to have become quite sober in the last few minutes. "Sir, I assure you of my eternal gratitude. Such a service . . ."

"Don't worry about thanking me," Arthur said uncomfortably. "I'd do the same for anybody—any spirit, I mean.

If it's okay with Maxton, I'll come around and see how you're settling in."

"Be assured that I for one will ever welcome you," said the ghost. "Good night, Arthur. May you sleep well, even when . . ."

He turned and faded into the wall.

For a long time Arthur stood on the doorstep. At last he turned and went back to the waiting cab, whose driver was half-asleep over his wheel. Happily he gave his address and drowsed in the back of the vehicle.

Apart from minor irritations, such as visits from a tenacious and unwelcome member of the Society for Psychical Research, James assured Arthur he was delighted with his new lodgings. He liked the Maxtons, and he got on splendidly with those of their friends who could be trusted not to noise the fact of his existence too widely abroad. All in all, he declared, he was nearer to paradise than at any previous time.

The winter set in, as cold as the summer had been hot, and pipes buried even in the depths of the ground cracked and split with the frost. Late one January evening Arthur was sitting huddled over an electric fire with three sweaters and his overcoat on, because the watermain had frozen and the central heating was out of action. He was deep in the analysis of a particularly knotty clause in a contract when there was a rustle behind him.

He turned to find a young woman in a full-skirted gown in the center of the room. Her neckline was spectacular, to say the least—even if both the bosom and the gown were silvery gray.

"Pray do not be alarmed at my unceremonious intrusion," said his visitor. "I am informed that you are Mr. Arthur Jordan, a lawyer. Is't so?"

Well, at any rate this time I have some clothes on, reflected Arthur. *And I can see why she turned James's head. Hmmm, ve-ery nice!*

Aloud he said, rising, "Mrs. Kitty Shaw, I believe! Won't you sit down?"

But when the pipes thawed, of course, she had to stop coming.

COINCIDENCE DAY

The sun rose over the rim of the ocean to tint the sky and also the domed roofs, pontoons and other visible surfaces of NASEEZ with a pearly pinkness. Nigel Stonerly paid no attention.

Time passed.

Certain mechanisms within the structure of NASEEZ stepped up their level of activity to full daytime intensity. Others, set to follow a different time schedule, ignored the arrival of a new local day. Nigel Stonerley, even without being adjusted to a different time schedule, copied the latter example.

Time passed.

Finally an alarm over the Stonerleys' double bed joined the roster of mechanisms responding to the sunny morning, and was in its turn disregarded. Nigel Stonerley was very good at disregarding the alarm.

Shortly, however, a determined elbow jabbed him in the ribs, and he had to come close enough to waking to resist the nudges. He put both arms around his petite, dark, power-packed wife, Midge, and uttered an optimistic grunt. Seven years of marriage enabled her to translate: "Five more minutes?"

"No," Midge told him, and prodded again. "Galaxy, Nigel! Why do you have to spend so much of your time asleep?"

"'M rehearsing," he mumbled. "Wanna adjust to a thirty-hour day like Chuckaluck had to get used to ours."

"Chuckaluck did his adjusting after he got here." Midge kicked out with bare toes. "Move, you inert blob of protoplasm! It's going to be a heavy day. Coincidence Days always are."

"Enough damned talent around this zoo to manage

without me for five more minutes . . ." But he rolled over and opened his eyes. "What degree of coincidence are we getting today, by the way?"

"You're the curator of this overgrown menagerie—you should know."

"You're the director of public relations—you get the figures out of the computer and dress 'em up pretty as bait for the be-lov-ed visitors." Nigel yawned.

Midge gave ground. After all, this, if anything, would haul her husband out of bed. "Ninety-nine and a half percent," she said sweetly.

"What?" Nigel jolted upright. The bed complained frantically as it tried to find where he had to go and adjust to a suitable support-pattern. "But you can't have half a—"

"Day. Chlamys III's day cycle overlaps and doesn't cut out until noon. So it's going to be a record-breaking morning."

"You win," Nigel sighed. He shouted at the shower to turn itself on warm. Midge overruled him.

"Cold!" she called. *"Ice-cold!"*

With a groan and a grim smile respectively, the Curator and the Public Relations Director of North America (Southeast) Extraterrestrial Zoo rose to face the alarming prospect of a Coincidence Day.

Chuckaluck roused from nostalgic dreams of paddling across the blyga fields by starlight, the aroma of crushed blossoms as vivid as reality in his olfactory cavities, and surveyed the accommodation where he was currently quartered. He was tightly inserted into a hollow redwood-tree stump he liked the scent of the dried wood, and a little patient work on his arrival had turned the hole in the middle into a very passable substitute for his bed at home. Practically everything else within the four walls of his cell was from the same place as himself: Agassiz IV. Huge, trailing clusters of bjao fruit dangled on the trellis masking the ceiling, dripping juice; frecatee leaves rustled to his left, nobmass stalks wove their ceaseless rhythms to his right. On Agassiz IV there was nowhere one could see bjao, frecatee and nobmass together on the same continent, let alone the same patch of ground. But Chuckaluck wasn't complaining. He had settled in very well here, and his hosts—keepers, whatever one called them—were kindly and considerate.

He emerged from his sleeping hole with a pop like a cork from a bottle. He was about the size of a large dog, covered with fine, close fur of a shade between russet and gold—a very attractive color, and one he often studied with approval in the mirror hidden behind the bjao trellis. He had three equally spaced lower limbs, affording him ambulation in any direction, and six upper limbs of great delicacy and sensitivity. The top of his body perceived color—in a range differing notably from the human, but shapes he detected chiefly by the use of a kind of sonar. His sense of smell was very highly evolved, thanks to the large, wet cavities under his upper limbs, through three of which he breathed.

He retired first behind a clump of ubel, also an import from Agassiz IV, and performed morning excretions and acts of self-maintenance. Then he extended his lower limbs to their maximum length and began to browse a breakfast off the bjao vines.

Madam Senior-Jones emerged from her own similar morning ritual—ablutions, cosmetinting, and certain other operations still more private but necessary before facing the world—and covered a yawn even though there was no one else in her luxurious apartment to be offended by a sight of her tonsils. The day stretched ahead of her, long, brilliant, and empty. She yawned again as she dropped into her breakfast chair and instructed it to issue her Meal One, Day Nine of her current diet chart.

Madam was her given name, not a title. Papa had been a stickler for the fitness of things. He had spent the greater part of a lifetime proving beyond reasonable doubt that his branch of the Jones family was the original one with which everyone else attempted to keep up; even after he adopted the hyphenated Senior in front of his name, however, other people resolutely refused to show him the deference due to a family tree of such eminence.

Fuming at the thought that his beloved daughter might have to go through life being treated like any ordinary person, he cast about for some means of insuring against this. Inspired by his own name—which was Adam, in

honor of his most distant forefather—he hit on the ingenious device of giving her the name she now bore; it
struck him as ideally appropriate, both because it rhymed
with his own and because it was a title so generally indica-
tive of superiority that it had been used even when
addressing queens.

On discovering, belatedly, the other main meaning of
the word, he died of shame and mortification. But he had
survived long enough to instill in the child a sense of the
fitness of things nearly as intense as his own, and she had
spent her entire, leisured, adult existence in setting right
things which were none of her concern.

The tiring campaign to have the shelf brackets in the
left aisle-store of the city library coppered instead of
chromed—more suitable to the genuine antique books in
that wing, some of which had cloth and even leather bind-
ings—had been successfully concluded two weeks before.
She had recovered more quickly than she had expected
from this immense expenditure of effort and had already
mentioned to her most intimate friends her desire to get
back to the swing of events soon. With much clucking of
tongues and wondering how she ever found the energy, they
then changed the subject.

Clearly, subjects for action were in short supply right
now.

The chair delivered the meal recommended by the diet
chart—maximum energy, minimum calories—and also,
to her surprise, an envelope bearing her address. She
couldn't remember when she had last received a message
other than via videophone; it was such a strain on most
people to compose words into grammatical sentences
with a writing machine, and so much more pleasant to sit
for an hour or two chatting with a colored image before
one to remind one to whom one was talking. . . .

She turned the envelope over, puzzled, and it opened
itself, dropping on her ample lap two enclosures. The
first was brief to the point of curtness, and ran simply:

> In view of the name you hear and the worthy
> opinions you hold on matters of public concern, I think
> you should see this and possibly take action!

There was no signature. But on studying the second enclosure, Madam Senior-Jones was quite prepared to forgive that. Why, even someone of her iron nerve would be shaken by the blatancy, the crudity, the savagery, the primitivism of it all!

Tears filled her eyes as she reflected how near this cause had been to dear Papa's heart, and how grossly she had dishonored his memory by letting the matter rest for so long. Why, it must be years since she had given a thought to the fate of our dumb cousins!

Resolution filled her, to such unprecedented effect that within two hours she had not only spoken to eight of her old campaigning associates—those who had proved most indefatigable in the library affair and others similar—but also dressed in an outfit about which she did not immediately change her mind and take it off.

She left her apartment and set off for NASEEZ, brandishing the offending second enclosure. It was a gaudy come-on pamphlet explaining about the record-breaking Coincidence Day.

NASEEZ was not a large zoo by twenty-fifth-century standards—nothing like Outback Australia or Siberia-Mars. It could boast no more than two or three thousand alien exhibits, grouped in some fifty presentations. But it was the best-attended zoo on Earth, for two excellent reasons: it was nearer to large centers of population than any other EZ, and it had been able to select those exhibits that were most interesting to the casual sightseer. Outback and Siberia, the purpose of whose existence was to conduct research into the biology and metabolism of the alien creatures they housed, were hard to get to and rather dull if one did bother to make the trip. Free of this particular obligation, NASEEZ had been able to organize its material far more attractively.

True, it was necessary to separate exhibits and visitors by physical barriers. Many of the aliens breathed chlorine, some cyanide, and few could tolerate more than one percent oxygen. This disadvantage was felt keenly by people who had been accustomed since childhood to riding lion-back, wrestling crocodiles and braiding rattlesnake necklaces—the common attractions at old-fashioned Terrestrial Zoos—and who expected to be able to do corresponding things with alien beasts at NASEEZ. Of course, oxygen-breathing creatures could be allowed to enter the immediate presence of visitors; one such at present in residence was Chuckaluck, and very popular he had proved.

Few people, however, left NAZEEZ disappointed, despite this drawback. A tour of the premises was made interesting by every possible device. Alien visual spectra, for instance, to one side or the other of the human range, allowed bizarre lighting effects, often brilliant ones, which the aliens did not perceive and hence were not bothered by. Lighting for exotic shadow shapes and hypnotic textures; fluctuation in the field strength of artificial gravities, giving a sensation of being on other planets; discreet aromas in the air circulators; microphones to relay the curious noises made by cell occupants—all resources were called into play.

Of course, what visitors saw was only the surface of NASEEZ. A moment's reflection, or turning the pages of the souvenir guidebook, or the recorded explanatory voice emerging at every corner of every passageway made that clear. Myriads of invisible mechanisms monitored the well-being of the creatures here. Atmosphere, temperature, gravity, food—this was only half the story. Some beings had digestive cycles dependent on temperature; some required special angles of illumination to prevent their developing anxiety neuroses; some could only excrete in response to special stimuli, lacking which they died rapidly of autointoxication. The list of matters attended to by the tireless machines was well-nigh endless.

Directly connected with such questions was the zoo's worst problem.

Some state of minimal activity corresponding to sleep occurred in the biocycle of all the highly organized creatures at NASEEZ. Visiting hours, naturally, had to be based on local (Earthside) time, but it was no help to anyone when those who came were confronted with a series of inert lumps, even if those lumps were fifty light-years from home.

Attempts were consequently always made to adapt the aliens to a twenty-four-hour day. Some adjusted easily;

others could not at any price, being too tightly fixated on their home world's night-day cycle.

During the ten hours a day when the zoo was open for visitors, as many as half the exhibits might be slumbrously dull. Alternatively, the cycles might chime together and the whole place become a buzz of vigorous movement, color and sound. The latter occasions always brought visitor in hordes because they were always well advertised. For convenience they had to have a name and a definition: a Coincidence Day was one when forty or more of the fifty presentations were at day-activity peak for at least five hours.

Today everything had hit at once. Even the fibrous creatures from Chlamys III would now repass the transition point between Ice IV and Ice V until after noon.

All records, and other things, were set to be broken.

"This is one busy day," Nigel muttered. For the past three hours he had been monitoring over the TV relays the ebb and flow of visitors along the tunnels, corridors and airy walkways of the zoo, like granulated blood-cell surrogates in some monster's circulatory system. He had also eavesdropped on the inane comments they were passing, and that was never an experience which endeared his own species to him.

"Admissions are at an all-time high," Midge confirmed. "I just read off the totals. But that's not what I wanted to tell you. Trouble's on the way."

"Said trouble being—?"

"The kind that runs in the Senior-Jones family. It has about seven or eight loyal associates at its heels."

Nigel winced, but rose to his feet. "I'll go tag along behind her party, then," he said. "Wish me luck."

"Speaking of luck," Midge said, taking his place at the TV monitors, "how's Chuckaluck today? Overexcited?"

"Not that it shows. More sort of . . . bored. Children *will* keep expecting to be given a ride on him, and he's not adapted." Nigel pulled a face and went out.

"Disgraceful!" Madam Senior-Jones thundered, and her companions chimed in dutifully in agreement. "Inhuman! Savage!"

Curious eyes turned on her. She promised to be even more entertaining than the creatures on show from distant worlds.

"To imprison living beings whose birthright is freedom, like ours! Would you wish to be shut up and stared at?"

"Awful. Disgusting. Ought to be a law," confirmed the breathless ladies at her heels.

From a short distance to the roar, Nigel watched with narrowed eyes. Over the various cells, the never-ending autocommentaries explained the nature of the exhibits.

". . . accustomed to gravity of five decimal four Earth-normal, temperature minus seventy degrees centigrade, atmosphere chiefly of hydrogen which is not utilized biologically, like the nitrogen in our own air, the active ingredient being . . ."

"To be taken—to be *ravished* from their familiar homes," Madam howled on. "Thrust into the dark and noisome hole and 'made a geck and gull—' "

Nigel didn't like having NASEEZ referred to as a noisome hole, but he did rather admire the Shakespearean quotation. He began mentally composing a limerick about Madam.

> "Her father, a man most intense,
> Literally spared no expense . . ."

Coming toward Chuckaluck's cell now, and the throng of people that always gathered there when he was out in the open, available for touching and—inevitably—smelling. He had a strong odor of his own, not unpleasant if you like aniseed mixed with ambergris.

> "To provide education
> Befitting her station . . ."

The crowd, predominantly juvenile, had pulled back in awe around Chuckaluck—not from him particularly, but from the man in spacecrew scarlet beside him. Some of the kids merely gazed admiringly, while others whispered among themselves and tried to work up the courage to ask for his thumbprint.

> "And with nothing so common as sense!"

Nigel took a deep breath as Madam charged up to the

man in scarlet and thrust a bony finger at him.

"Are you one of the dastards who tear these miserable creatures from the bosom of their parent worlds and make them a spectacle for idle, heartless thrill-seekers?"

One or two of her companions had doubts about the word "dastard," but only muttered to themselves. Madam was magnificently in command.

The spaceman looked her over and straightened from the low plinth on which he had been leaning. "Navigator Laban Howe, at your service," he said in a gentle drawl. "Would you mind repeating your question?"

"I said—oh, you heard me perfectly well!" Madam had hit optimum pitch now and was staying on it. "You've come to gloat over the fruits of your evil labor! Creating misery and casting into bondage creatures which, though they have not the fortune to be born on Earth, are at least living beings with rights and—"

Chuckaluck was yielding to excitement now, Nigel could tell by the way his upper limbs twitched, especially the ones under which were his three breathing orifices.

Navigator Howe caught the attention of the amused crowd gathered behind Madam and gave it an enormous sidelong wink that provoked anticipatory grins. "Matter of fact," he stated in a casual tone, "I came to say hullo to Chuckaluck here, see how he's getting along. He tells me he's fine."

"He—*tells* you?" echoed Madam, almost choking with passion.

"Why, sure!" The voice full of innocence, but another big wink in case the audience missed the point the first time. "I visited Agassiz a couple of time, and Chuckaluck and me, we understand each other pretty well."

"*Shame!*" screamed Madam as soon as she could take a breath deep enough to match the depth of her feelings. "To exhibit brute beasts and pander to the sensation-seeking no-goods of our decadent modern age—that's bad enough. But to place a creature here to whom has been accorded the divine gift of speech . . . !" She raised both fists. "Who's in charge of this monstrous, disgusting, inhuman prison?"

Nigel sighed and pushed his way through her train of clucking biddies. "I am the curator of this zoo," he said in a firm voice, "and I must require you to leave the precincts at once. You are causing a disturbance and interfering with the peaceful enjoyment of other visitors."

For two and a half minutes she told him what she thought of this kind of enjoyment. When she paused, he said, as though there had been no interruption, "Or else I shall send for the police and have you physically removed from the zoo."

Two hours laters the police came. For him and Chuckaluck. While they were waiting, Midge had performed some speculative calculations, addressing the air rather than Nigel.

"Well, it'll take her one hour to finish expressing her opinion of Nigel Stonerley, the infamous tyrant and public enemy, and another hour to work out the constructive paths of action. Her first impulse will be to video her Pan-Solar congressman—"

"I hope to goodness she doesn't," muttered Nigel. "Egremont Sissoko is the last person I'd want here right now."

"Should have thought of that earlier. Well, maybe she skipped that and went to stage two: contact the local news services. Stage three will be to find the mayor and chief of police and lay a complaint against you. Two hours."

Correct—and the police came, in a puzzled frame of mind, but armed with a John Doe warrant and a list of possible charges, including kidnapping, unlawful detention, and slander. (The last was a gallant shot in the dark by one of Madam's colleagues, widow of a lawyer whom she had worked into an early grave, and who did her best to cope with Madam's fits of annoyance when she felt "there oughta be" but wasn't "a law.")

"Is this thing okay the way he is?" the sergeant of police inquired, eyeing Chuckaluck's gold and russet form with some diffidence. "Shouldn't he to be on a lead or something?"

"Chuckaluck has never been involved in any trouble since he came here," Midge snapped. "And if it wasn't for that silly woman, he wouldn't be involved in any now."

"I guess not," the sergeant sighed, and moved toward the window at which the squad floater waited.

News today must be scanty, Nigel realized. Several news chains had had the bright idea of picking up this oddball story and giving it silly-season prominence, and headlines blared at them as they approached the courtroom through a horde of camereyes, mikears, and extensosensors.

"WHO'S ZOO? IT'S A GAS SAYS AGASSIZ! SERIOUS CHARGE AG'ST CURATOR, NASEEZ."

And so on.

Waiting in the court, looking righteous, were Madam and her group of instant campaigners. Someone either on her list of contacts or else—more likely—on the court's advisory staff had done some quick research, because, when Judge Corcoran entered to take his place on the bench, he proved not to be sitting alone, but with two assessors, the standard procedure to determine whether a bill would lie. The one on his right was human: a provincial senator from NAPROV Congressenate. The one on his left was a featureless metal cylinder with extensosensors angled up from its top.

The public seating was crammed; videoceptors and other newsgathering devices filled every row. The air was as taut as overstrained elastic.

"Right!" said the judge when everyone had stared his or her fill of Chuckaluck, seated after the fashion of his species on the most suitable article the premises could offer, a large wastebin. "I'm Judge Corcoran, sitting with assessors here to determine whether an offense has been committed against the general tenor and spirit of Solar System justice, there being no specific statute—"

"Yes, there is!" Madam interrupted. "I sent you three—"

"Silence," the judge said. "Yes, you sent me three, and I've incorporated them in the hypothetical indictment—"

"There's nothing hypothetical about what's been done to this poor creature," Madam said firmly, and clamped her mouth shut.

"Er. Yes." Judge Corcoran studied Chuckaluck briefly and gave a shrug. "As to identities of parties to the action: you're Nigel Stonerley, correct? Curator of NASEEZ? Mm-hm. Well, you're indicted conjointly with those who have aided and abetted the bringing from Agassiz IV of the creature known as Chuckaluck, especially Navigator Laban Howe of the Interstellar Service. Uh . . . as to Chuckaluck: *is* that his name?"

"It's as near as most people can come to pronouncing it."

"I see. And can he understand these proceedings?"

"Oh, sure he can." Nigel blinked. "What he can't understand, he says, is the point of them."

"Shame on you!" Madam bellowed across the court. "Putting lies into the mouth of a brute beast to—"

She broke off, eyes widening, just as Corcoran banged his gavel and ordered her to be silent.

"You shouldn't be so hard on the lady," admonished the human assessor, the provincial senator. He was dimly aware that organizing women like Madam were a power in the land hereabouts, and had some notion that she might put votes his way at the next election.

"Thank you!" Madam acknowledged. "It's a pleasure to know someone present enjoys natural human tenderness and compassion."

The robot assessor signaled for attention and said in its grating voice, "Precedent shows that emotion clouds the true evaluation of facts. Judge is directed to note that my assessment is not confused by bias of compassion."

Looking harassed, Corcoran said, "Yes . . . ah . . . thank you. Well now, as I was saying earlier: no statute is clearly applicable but the law recognizes that we live in an evolving universe and permits the device of a hypothetical indictment to see if an action is contrary to the tenor of natural justice and—"

"You've just heard him admit it," Madam broke in.

"Ah—what?" By now Corcoran was wishing the case had fallen to anyone but himself.

"He admitted it, when he said Chuckaluck understands what's going on!" Madam leaned forward intensely. "He's kept a speech-gifted being in miserable captivity, in *durance vile* in his abominable zoo—which ought to be closed down anyway, ought never to have been opened and wouldn't have been if my lamented papa had had his way—disgusting to pen living creatures into cages and cells and let the common ruck and run go gawp and gape at—"

"What is this farce?" said a measured voice from the doorway of the courtroom.

All heads turned. A thickset man stood there, scowling, his polished bald head reflecting the lights in the ceiling. There was no mistaking the celebrated NASE delegate to the Pan-Solar Congress, Egremont Sissoko.

"Why, Congressman!" Madam exclaimed delightedly. "How good, how kind of you to answer my call so promptly! How—"

"Shut up, you silly woman," Sissoko said, and the words left her gasping for air, exactly like a gaffed fish, mouth working but no sound emerging. "Well, Nigel?" he added to the curator of NASEEZ. "I suppose you chose this particular day because I was away from the Capitol, and it never struck you that I might be coming to look over my bailiwick rather than taking a vacation!"

Nigel, looking almost as miserable as Madam, shook his head. "It's Coincidence Day, that's all. It's purely a coincidence that—"

"Coincidences hell!" Sissoko said briskly. "All right, Judge, clear the court and I'll explain. Or—damnation, why should I bother clearing the court? It's only going to kick up rumors."

"Thank you," Corcoran said with some dignity. "This is after all *my* court, and telling me to clear it is close to contempt."

"Oh, the contempt has been on someone else's part," Sissoko snorted. He strode up to the bench and whispered, too low for the news services to pick up; even the robot assessor had to crane close with its extensosensors.

Then it said loudly, "Information confirms tentative opinion. Gross infringement of privilege. Recommend arrest of Madam Senior-Jones and associates as public nuisances and disturbers of the peace—"

It took the judge that long to shut off its speech circuits. The shock was too much for Madam; she keeled over in a dead faint.

"That's carrying things a bit far," Sissoko grunted. "I guess we can leave it at that. Okay, boys and girls!" he added to the news services. "Break it up. All finished. If you haven't figured it out yet, go look up Senior-Jones in the *Record of Digest Biography* and read about his campaign to prevent NASEEZ being built."

It might occur to them to wonder about the robot's choice of the phrase "gross infringement of privilege," but so long as they didn't hit on the right explanation for that, things were all in order.

"I'm terribly sorry, Chuckaluck," Nigel said in halting Agassizian as they reentered the office from which he kept watch on the zoo. "It's going to spoil your thesis, isn't it, having the campaign cut short in this way?"

Chuckaluck laid a comforting upper limb on Nigel's shoulder and uttered a wheeing reply, meaning approximately, "Never mind. Even from this brief experience I have garnered clues to many things that mystified me beforehand."

Nigel, wondering whether this was kindliness or the truth, gave a grateful smile nonetheless, and looked around the room. His smile vanished. Instead of finding only Midge, he was confronted with a thunderous-looking Sissoko.

"Now you two have some explaining to do," Sissoko barked. "Come on, out with it! What's the real story? I told the judge it was part of the Senior-Jones campaign against NASEEZ and motivation by malice would be proved easily—you were just stringing along to get the publicity, which was disgraceful."

"No, I promise you it was done with the best intentions," Chuckaluck wheed. Nigel translated, and looked earnestly at Sissoko.

"Congressman, Chuckaluck has been doing a study, ever since his arrival, of campaigns in human society—how grievances and complaints get taken up by organized bodies of people and how the process is brought to a conclusion in or not in the form of action. Well, of course, he's had plenty of secondhand information, but he's never been directly involved in such a campaign.

"It—uh—worried Midge and me, because, after all, it's Agassiz IV where we're going to serve our time as zoo specimens, and we wanted to do as much as possible for him. Then we hit on a solution by a lucky coincidence."

"I'm hearing too damned much about coincidence!" growled Sissoko.

"Well, this *was* one." Midge turned defiant eyes on him. "A Coincidence Day here meant that we were distributing a lot of publicity anyway, and we heard that the most vocal local—I mean—oh, the *hell*: vocal local is what she is—professional-amateur campaign-forcer was at a loose end. It involved nothing more on our part than sending her a copy of our pamphlet and an unsigned letter urging action. We were sure an oblique reference to her family name would trigger the response we wanted."

"We happened—uh—yes, we just *happened* to have heard from Laban Howe to say he wanted to call on Chuckaluck before lifting for space again." Nigel combed his hair with nervous fingers. "So we persuaded him to meet the Madam if it could be arranged—which it could —and he played his part to perfection."

"Blazes, don't sound so smug!" Sissoko blasted them. "You took the most damnable risks! What do you think would have happened if it had come out in open court that you, so-called curator of NASEEZ, have no more power over the place than I have—that it's a cooperative run by its inhabitants and the staff jobs are given to volunteers bound for zoos on other planets? Hey?"

"It wouldn't have come out," Nigel muttered. "I'd arranged for—"

"What *you'd* arranged resulted in the concentrated attention of every news service in the province," Sissoko cut in. "I wish we didn't have to run a zoo anyway! It's a thin cover at best."

"But very useful," wheed Chuckaluck. "One could hardly expect humans to act naturally in the presence of spacesuited visitors, if we were to go among you to conduct our social studies of your species. Thinking themselves only in the presence of their own kind and unintelligent—hence uncritical—animals, they relax and act unaffectedly."

"Granted," Sissoko agreed when Nigel translated. "But —all right, you tell me, then. What were you going to do to prevent the truth from emerging and wrecking a century of hard work?" He mopped his face. "I can just imagine that stupid provincial senator sitting up, all self-important, and shooting off his mouth about 'deceit and trickery and dishonest dealings' and, 'anyway, humans shouldn't be exposed to such scrutiny' and 'young man, are you trying to tell me you have *volunteered* to demean your dignity as a human being by offering to go and be a—a—a—?' "

His parody of helpless astonishment and righteous indignation was so effective even he found he was grinning at the end of it.

"As it so happens," Midge chuckled, "I have right here an example of what we were going to do to prevent such ideas getting about." She tapped open a drawer and handed a sheet of gaudy paper to Sissoko.

It looked like, but wasn't, a photo. It was an offset three-dee drawing in full color of an easily recognizable spot within NASEEZ, but shown from within the exhibits' cells. Beyond the barriers shutting off the cells, but fully visible, were people, and all of them had a subtle but noticeable resemblance to Madam Senior-Jones.

"That's the pamphlet for our next Coincidence Day," Midge explained. "Or will be, when text is added. You'll notice that the illusion is given of looking into the public areas from the cells, of the roles being reversed—does it affect you? We spent a long time getting it right!"

"Oh, yes." Sissoko was chortling. "Perfect, perfect! Show people the truth the right way, and they'll never believe it. Right here is the way things are—aliens studying people in the zoo—and not one person who sees this will think of anything but that Madam made a fool of her species by saying they were penning up an intelligent being." He tossed the picture on the table.

"Okay, you're forgiven. But I hope the next curator has fewer bright ideas. The sooner you're safely shut up in a zoo on Agassiz IV, the better I'll be pleased."

WHIRLIGIG

And for the last time, Spinks, *I* am telling *you* that we *are* going to include "Gumshoe Stumble" in our next recording session whether you like it or not! And you're going to release it as a single immediately, and I'm going to see that label say big and bold and clear: " 'Gumshoe Stumble' by Tommy Caxton and his Solid Six." Get me?

No, next time won't *do*—I want the present band to put it down. Louie's finally getting hitched to his girl Cindy, and Alf Reardon's joining Stumpy Biggleman for his tour of Egypt, and I—

No, I *won't* shut up and I *won't* think it over and I *am* being reasonable! And I'll talk like that to you or any other A&R man in the business until I manage to get this simple, plain, straightforward fact through your head. Listen carefully: we are going to record that number and you are going to release it. Is that clear, or do I have to get a hot poker and write it on your—uh—?

I've already told you, Goddamit! I know perfectly well there's an Icky Black version and one by Buck Milligan *and* one by Benny Call! I *know* there's no future in covering an Icky Black disc. But there's absolutely and positively no future in not recording—

Oh, to hell with it. Give me a cigarette and let me get my breath back. I guess I'll have to tell you the whole story, though I'm damned sure you won't believe a word of it.

Listen, you know Nick Barelli? Used to run the Crypt Club near Marble Arch until that time when—uh—well, until the word got around and nobody would play the joint for a million. That's him. Well, after the club went broke, I felt sort of it was my fault and a bit guilty, and anyway, I did him a few favors and now he's back on his feet, he tries to do me a few in return. Well, the other evening he gives me a buzz and says have you an evening free next week because I have a good gig for your band. So I say, how about Wednesday, and he covers the phone and I wait and he comes back after a few minutes and says great, Wednesday it is and how do you feel about a hundred and fifty and expenses for a four-hour stint at a big society do?

Right there I should have spotted something fishy. I mean, what kind of a society function is it where the date depends on whether you can get the band that night? But I hadn't any mind to spare for that question. I was wondering whether I liked a hundred and fifty smackers plus exes more than I hated swank society parties. I mean, last time we'd played one there was this louse who called Fats Hamilton a big buck nigger, and Fats got so mad, he learned the guy's name and went in the toilet and drew a picture four feet high with lipstick all over the wall and wrote the name underneath. I guess I better hadn't say what he'd drawn the guy doing. But we won't be booked into that joint again.

So I tried to get some more details out of Nick. But all I learned was the guy's name—Mister Mordecai Smith—and the tone of voice Nick used to say "Mister" sort of smelled like money burning and meant make up your mind fast, he could have Icky Black instead. So I said okay, where is this show? He says vaguely it's out of town somewhere, and goes off the line for another minute or two. Finally he comes back to say the guy who's hiring us will provide his own transport and bring us home afterward.

Now, this is even odder. Most people wouldn't soil their limousines with a musician's hind end, so we have this minibus arrangement with back seats that turn into bunks and a compartment in the roof where you can put the horns even when it's snowing, and besides we like using it because it has this slogan of Alf's painted on the back—"YOU ARE FOLLOWING TOMMY CAXTON'S SOLID SIX, WHY NOT CATCH US SOME TIME?" And so on. So I argue. So Nick wins.

Or rather, he drives it through my head that Mister Mordecai Smith is the kind of guy who prefers his own ideas even if they're bad ones. So okay. All fixed for Wednesday, they collect us at six-thirty outside Nick's office and take us home to our own pads after. We all live close together, but even so, when we chew the facts over afterward, the only one we really like is the rate for the job.

Still, I wasn't too worried. Not till I showed on Wednesday as agreed, and here's Nick with all the boys except Ed—bass, you know? There's some sort of argument going on with Louie Ditton, my clarinetist. I get the drift. He wants to take Cindy along as usual, who's standing there looking bored, and Nick is saying Mister Smith wouldn't like it and in fact positively forbade it, and in the interests of band discipline—what we have of it, but who'd want to lose it completely?—I come in on Nick's side.

Why the hell not take Cindy? Louie says. Look, there's room in those things for a small army! And he points across the road to where there's two cars waiting, with a couple of uniformed shovers sort of tapping their fingers on the weheels.

I do a double take. What the blazes are those is what I want to know! And Bill Sandler, our piano man, who's a car buff, takes me literally and says that's one Rolls-Royce Silver Ghost and one Hispano-Suiza eight-passenger limousine weighing about two tons and built like a tank and that's Mister Smith's transport and it's *beautiful*.

Still, even though Louie's right about the small army, Nick is right about Mister Smith, and I say so. So Louie says to Nick in no uncertain terms he wants to know who this vest-pocket dictator is, anyway!

Matter of fact, that's something we'd all like to know, so we turn the codfish eye on Nick, and he goes all Italian and helpless and all he can say is the guy turned up and asked for our band, which he had the name of in a notebook with him, and there was this sort of rare alligator binding on the notebook, and he was dressed *but* magnificently and had these rings dripping from his fingers and a whole squad of private secretaries and such dancing around, and if we wanted to see our pay, we'd better get in those cars!

So Ed shows up just then, apologizing—he has this mini-minor and the most overgrown bass you ever saw,

and some trouble with the roof rack, or something. . . .
Anyway, time's running out and I have no choice but to
come the heavy father and tell Louie Cindy doesn't ride,
and everyone else tells him to shut up and get in because
it's brass-monkey weather and Cindy says what she thinks
of Mister Smith and beats it, and that's that.

Now we find out the shovers are as weird as their cars.
I mean, did you ever see a car with a clock in the middle
of the steering wheel? Bill says it's an eighty-day stopwatch,
but I think Big Ben pupped the week the thing left the
factory. I—no, that's not what I started to say. Here
these two shovers just sit watching us struggle with the
instruments, not making a move to help, more sort of
hoping the strain will kill us. Well, this gets Alf Reardon
down, of course—he doesn't like people who think musicians are an inferior species. I keep him quiet for a bit,
and we climb in, and then Fats wants to know where we're
going. He asks me. I say, hell, I don't know, ask the
shover!

And the shover sneers and slams the door and off we go.

Well, with a chance to sit back and think, I'm frowning
till my forehead feels like corrugated paper. We don't
know where we're going, I haven't seen the guy who hired
us, Alf is bloody-minded about the shover and vice versa,
and the general feeling is, Tommy, are you off your
marble to get us mixed up in this? I am not happy, believe
me.

Still, we cool down, and Fats passes a jar of rum,
which normally I wouldn't allow on the way to this sort
of function—not after the episode of the picture in the
gents—but I figure Alf's halfway right and we aren't
going to be treated like royalty, so why behave like it?

Some time around when it gets dark, I look out the back
for the second car following us, and I yell. And so do the
others. Here, so help me, since we last paid any mind to
the outside world, a fog's blown up so thick and black
you can't see a yard out of the window, and here's this
crazy driver pouring on the coal like high noon in midsummer.

So I bash the glass partition, and the shover picks up one
of these real speaking-tube things, you know? And he
says in an upper-crust voice something about no need to

be alarmed, *gentlemen,* this is only a patch of mist, and the words come out all echoing and hollow. Fats grabs his jar of rum back from Bill, and while he's still gulping, the shover turns out to be right and here we are, pulling up a concrete driveway outside a monstrous great country mansion yea long by yea tall.

Like wow! says Ed. But there's not time to take in the view—here comes a stinking-rich-looking character surrounded by flunkies and monkeys and alongside him a girl like—like—oh, I'll save my breath. She was just unbelievable all the way down from her coal-black hair to her—never mind. What I mean, you could hear eyes popping like champagne corks.

So I say, Mister Mordecai Smith? And kick Louie on the shin to tell him he might as well stop preening himself, who looks at musicians in this class of joint except nymphos going slumming? I have a good kick which means that. I have to use it on Louie all the time.

He says yes, and he is very gracious and glad to see us arrived safely, and trusts we will spend an enjoyable evening and this here is his daughter Galena, whose birthday party it is we've been engaged for.

So Galena takes my hand and holds it and looks at me and says are you *really* Tommy Caxton and I have *all* your records and it's *wonderful* having you actually playing at my party. And I suddenly think maybe I was wrong in the way I'd kicked Louie and I ought to have made it one of my ordinary keep-your-hands-off-or-I'll-tell-Cindy kicks.

Because this kid has eyes that you look deep, deep down into, like hotel corridors, and all the signs say with no chance of error, "BEDROOM."

I gulp, I nod. I look at Mister Smith, expecting him to throw me right back in the car. But no. He says about seeing to his guests and looking forward to hearing our music and this particular flunky out of all of them will take charge of us.

And before we've quite recovered, we've been processed with assembly-line efficiency through a small room where we get a chance to comb the hair and tune up, and we're on.

Jesus! From the size of the house, I'd expected a big

room, but this was a stadium! The daïs they put us on
would have accepted a symphony orchestra for a start,
and all it held was a half-dozen chairs, a Steinway grand
—Bill said it had a very stiff action, but maybe they didn't
want a jazzman beating hell out of a good piano—and us.

And over the edge of this football field we were on,
there were the people. They . . .

Now, look. Put yourself in our place. Here's this crazy
barn laid out with long white tables for bars and buffets,
barmen in white jackets, drinks flowing like water, and
this gang of more handsome men and more beautiful
women of all ages from chicks to hens than I ever saw in
my life—and I've played for the judging at Miss Europe
contests! And their *clothes*!

The women's were pretty much okay. I mean, I
didn't think in a setting like this you'd see the sack line and
the trapeze line and the A-line and the H-line and the god-
knows line all together, skirts all the way from the floor to
the hips, bosoms all the way from overexposed to underde-
veloped. But—hell, it was the men that bugged me. Some
were in evening dress that didn't fit. Some wore tartan
jackets and tight pants like army mess-dress. Some wore
tweed jackets of every shade from orange to blue. Some
wore ruffled shirts. Some—oh, I can't remember the lot.

Anyway, there wasn't time to look the scene over. Because here comes little Galena bouncing with excitement
—I didn't notice what she was wearing, but there wasn't
much of it—and this string of young men pinker-faced
and slicker-built than Guards officers, and dressed like
blitz victims. Charges up to the stand and waits, like
breathless, for us to start.

So I start. What else?

I stomp off a nice rousing opener—"Rampart Street."
Galena listens. Some of the other people move to the far
end, where I doubt if they can hear our triple forte. Some
ignore us. Some come and look us over the way squares
always do. I call it the "aquarium look." Only Galena
hangs on our every note, and her boyfriends stay put,
hanging on her.

Well, we play an hour and a half, and Smith sends to
say there's refreshments for the band and we may take up
to forty minutes before resuming if we wish. We wish,

all right. I guess I shouldn't admit it, but with Galena's melting eyes on me, I've been putting the band through Hoops. All our best numbers, all the toughies and the flag-wavers and the soulful blues one inch this side of corny, and Galena standing there like I was Gabriel.

And when she says how much she's enjoying the music, and *looks*, I know very well there's refreshment for the bandleader waiting somewhere—uh—private.

Maybe it was the Gabriel bit that put me off. I have personal reasons. Anyway, I didn't bite. I went off with the boys to the room behind the stand.

There's salad and smoked salmon and canapés and some wine I don't recognize, and white-jacketed waiters to serve us, and all this makes even Alf feel a bit less out of sorts. We sit around, eat, drink, light up and swap impressions. One impression is shared: this joint is the weirdest. The waiters don't help, either. They're as uncommunicative as the shovers.

Suddenly I notice something, and push my chair back. Where—is—Louie?

I'd seen him slip away, but I'd figured on doing the same before going back on the stand, and assumed the obvious reason. Only the obvious reason doesn't take twenty-five minutes.

Hmmm . . .

I get up, asking Bill which door, and he points, and a waiter opens for me and says to go to the end of the corridor. Some corridor. All white, with a springy floor. From one side of it rises—get this—an escalator. And something else odd: no lights. The light comes from everywhere. Poppa Mordecai's fortune obviously has several more zeroes than I first thought.

But anyway, what strikes me most is the piped music, which I can hear out here and couldn't in the room where we were eating. Very odd piped music. It bothers me all the time I'm in the john.

Because it sounds like a very old, crackly, scratchy 78, and I know damned well it's not. It's a track from a perfectly good new LP, by yours truly and his Solid Six, and a fan of mine as devoted as Galena has no business playing it in this condition. I mean, hell, she *must* be devoted. She's not satisfied with having her pop spend the cost of a hundred LP's to get us to her party—apparently she wants to hear us through the intermission, too.

And then, just as I'm coming back past the foot of the escalator, everything stops. There's a pause in the piped music, a scraping as the stylus picks up on a new disc, and a band goes into "Gumshoe Stumble," also with scratches and crackling.

MY BAND!

Jesus, I've played with Louis and Alf for years. I *knew* that was Alf's tram growling in there. I *knew* it was Louie codding around with those high-register squeaks. And most definitely of all I knew my own trumpet lead.

But I'd played "Gumshoe Stumble" so few times I could practically count them! We hadn't even played it this evening, and sure as hell we'd never cut a disc of it. So where did Galena get that recording?

I figured I'd been through the only door Louie would have been sent through. He wasn't in the can. That left the escalator. I put two and Galena together and hoped.

I was right.

This escalator starts by throwing me at a blank wall. Only suddenly it's not. It's a door, opened like a conjuring trick.

Here's this room, beautiful mother-of-pearl walls, spongy sea-green floor, furniture like—but I didn't see that in detail. I saw three things in detail. A record player, so old its wooden cabinet had wormholes in it and the veneer was cracked. Galena, making bedroom eyes, and Louie, so besotted he hadn't even caught on to what was happening.

Me, I screamed. No, maybe I yelled. I hope. I headed for the record player before Louie could jump—and fell bass over treble because I'd caught my foot in an electric cord that ran from the record player to the piped music system . . . I guess. So there I was flat on my face, with Louie blasting me under his breath and Galena hooting with laughter. I didn't care. I didn't like her any more. She scared me blue.

I scrambled up and grabbed the record off the player. I made Louie read the label. I never saw anyone go so white. He clutches his beard, he looks at Galena like a rattlesnake, and then he and I beat each other to the door. I dropped the record. It broke, I guess.

Because while we're running down the escalator hollering to be let out of here, Galena lets go a howl fit to lift the roof and we hear some of what she thinks about the way we treat her precious antiques.

Yes, I said antiques! She screamed it right out loud after us. She'd decided to give her living doll a treat, so she'd got out her genuine original discs, and that one I'd dropped—according to her—was *five hundred years old*.

We spoiled her birthday party, and Poppa Mordecai was sore as hell. He'd gone to a lot of trouble, like making the guests dress up in period so we wouldn't catch on, and hauling those cars out of maybe a museum some place. But that was just the half of it. *I* think he must have bent the law to swing the deal at all. I mean, if it wasn't illegal, we'd be hearing about it all the—

Spinks! Put that phone down! I'm not crazy! I'm just explaining why it's absolutely essential that we cut a disc of "Gumshoe Stumble" and . . .

GALACTIC CONSUMER REPORT NO. 3:

A SURVEY OF THE
MEMBERSHIP

*(Extract from GOOD BUY, the journal of the
Consolidated Galactic Federation of Consumers'
Associations, February 2330 ESY)*

Elsewhere in this issue you will find the complete results
of our questionnaire intended to discover exactly who (or
what) are our current members, why they joined, whether
they are satisfied with our service, and what products
you whom we are here to serve want us to test in the
immediate future. Owing to circumstances beyond our
control, some of which are set out below in the most
temperate language of which we are at present capable,
most of the data are primarily of academic or historical
interest now, but we can at least pride ourselves on the fact
that no similar undertaking has ever before been attempted, even though we could not in honesty advise anyone else to try it again.

When we first circulated the questionnaire, eight years
ago, we promised that its findings would appear in one
of the regular issues of this journal. We have managed to
keep that promise. The information is condensed in microdot form as the last full stop on the last page of the comparative study of high-precision microdot decipherers,
and both the items nominated as Best Buys will enable you
to read it, the magnification required being only of the
order of x 1,000,000.

Subscribers to the deluxe edition (apart from the two
members on Alpheratz IX who withheld seventeen credits
from their dues on the grounds that they are anyway capable of distinguishing individual molecules with the naked
eye) will eventually be sent the book version of the report.
However, we must warn them that, since it runs to
twenty-three fat volumes occupying a meter and a half

of shelf space, under current galactic mailing regulations it can only be shipped by uncrewed ion-rocket; consequently only members belonging to species of exceptional longevity can expect to receive their copies personally. The rest will have to be satisfied with bequeathing them to their grandchildren.

Doubtless, by now you're asking: "How did this delay arise?" Well, to start with, the level of response exceeded not only our wildest expectations but also those of the computer we hired to assess the likely return. It advised us that not more than one per million of the membership would be bothered to fill out such a complex form.

What we *in fact* got back was more like a sixty-seven percent response. As, relying on the computer's assessment, we had done no more by way of preparation than rent a small room in downtown Buenos Aires and hire an elderly female clerk with a hand-operated punch-card analyzer, the sudden arrival of 2,619,312,003 questionnaires caused a minor technical hitch.

By the way, in a future issue we propose to conduct a survey of commercial computer-advice services. Meantime, we must caution you against employing the Buckingham and Ketshwayo Service for Honest Oracular Pronouncements, which our staff is now accustomed to refer to as Bucket Shop. They are not, on present evidence, a "Good Buy."

We are also, incidentally, anxious to recruit volunteers to help us in a survey of planetside postal services. We feel it is high time to establish a Galactic Postal Convention to assure the private correspondence of any intelligent organism whatever proper protection in transit and reasonable speed of delivery. The treatment we have been accorded by the Earthside authorities beggars belief, and it is highly probable that some of the questionnaires which members on outlying planets went to a lot of trouble to complete and forward have never reached us.

For example, we regard it as inexcusable that merely because the only type of stationery available to a citizen of Shalimar happens to be fresh water-lily leaves and pale green bog slime instead of paper and ink, some jumped-up jack-in-office at the Galactic Mail Center in Lhasa should be allowed to class his envelope as "perishable foodstuffs improperly packaged" and decline responsibility for its delivery.

Furthermore, it's mere common civility on Toothanclaw to wrap any missive to a person one wishes to flatter or defer to in the hide of one's latest kill. The more ambitious the kill (and there are creatures on that planet none of our staff would care to handle without battle armor and a lase gun!), the greater the respect which the writer expresses toward the recipient.

One of our members there, obviously extremely appreciative of the services of ConGalFedConAss, chose to employ the hide of a mugglebuck in which to return his questionnaire. That this hide continues to secrete pure hydrofluoric acid for nine years after being flayed, we submit, is as nothing beside the basic requirement that it be delivered to the address inscribed on the outside. The fact that mugglebuck skin remains dangerous to handle after the animal is killed is essentially a symbolic equivalent of the customary salutation "Your humble and obedient servant," but no postal authority would decline to accept mail because it included that phrase!

It was only by chance that we received the questionnaire sent up by a member on Caligula, moreover. She had gone to enormous trouble to address her package, because the yoggoth worms there customarily employed for the purpose have been selectively bred to adopt the forms of the Devanagari alphabet rather than the Terrestrial Roman system; it must have required several months of patient labor to train them to display an Earthside address code.

All this nearly went for nothing when the Health Department sterilized the worms with insecticide—whereupon, of course, they reverted to the post-mortem straight position. Had it not been for an observant staff member who was visiting the post office on another errand altogether, that questionnaire would doubtless have gone into the dead-letter file.

But the last straw was the authorities' refusal to allow one of our members on Hydatia to answer our questionnaire at all—a flagrant example of bureaucratic censorship at its worst. Much as we dislike expending our funds on litigation, we feel that in this case there is an important point of principle at stake, and have instituted proceedings in the cause of interplanetary tolerance.

Hydatians do possess a written language, but they reserve it entirely for public inscriptions, advertising puffs and other works of fiction. The only form of private communication expressed in writing is an invitation to a duel to the death, so great an insult is it not to convey your messages in person.

Wishing to reply to our questionnaire, our member there adopted the normal course and put himself into suspended animation after attaching address labels and sufficient postage to his left ear. On arrival at our office, he would have delivered the information he had imprinted on his mind, and relapsed into his comatose state until restored to his home swamp.

However, despite being properly stamped for both the outward and return journeys, our member was forbidden admission to Earth—first by the Customs and Excise, which proposed to classify him as a museum exhibit subject to arbitrary valuation and five-hundred percent duty; then, when we'd sorted that out, by the Immigration Service, which argued that he lacked a visa.

Without being delivered, of course, the poor fellow will never wake up from his trance, so merely shipping him home doesn't solve the problem. A test case is now in progress before the Appellate Tribunal of the Pan-Galactic Court, and we will keep you apprised of developments.

Meantime, if anyone can offer us storage space for one inert male Hydatian approximately thirty-seven meters by eleven by four, capable of being maintained at a pressure of 325 kg./sq. cm. at −120° C., we would be obliged. At present we are having to pay rent on a bonded warehouse at a rate which promises that we shall go bankrupt around the second week of August.

We had hoped that one of the things this questionnaire would enable us to do is to revolutionize our method of selecting products to be tested by insuring that the items we choose are all goods that the members are eager to know about.

We have no wish to appear unappreciative of all the trouble you went to, but the sad truth is that after processing, cataloguing, and analyzing the various products suggested by a substantial number of our members (arbitrarily, one million or more), we have decided to keep right on the way we have been going already.

You see, the largest single batch of requests for tests on a single type of product which we received came from Triskelion. We had 8,623,517 of them. (Curiously enough, this was exactly the book strength of the Hawk party in the Archducy of Axenheim at the time our questionnaires arrived there.)

But we simply haven't got the facilities to evaluate the comparative merits of the various brands of planet-busting bomb at present on the market! We feel that if the Hawk party wish to substantiate its election slogan ("More Crash for a Credit!") they should institute their own testing program, preferably well away from Galactic trade routes.

We moreover feel very strongly that the two million-odd inquirers from Phagia who asked us to test them for edibility ought to set up their own planetary chapter of ConGalFedConAss. We cannot possibly hope to determine which of them will prove tastiest at his or her funeral feast—a matter of fierce rivalry among that species, in case you didn't know. Our entire permanent staff is human, and sampling creatures who live in an atmosphere of hydrogen sulfide at the boiling point of water would give us acute food poisoning, thus hopelessly biasing the results.

By the way, we have exercised our discretionary right to terminate membership in the case of the young lady from Hippodamia who asked us to test the thirty-seven men who are suing for her hand in marriage. Frivolity of this kind is not in keeping with the high ideals of our organization. And we would have done the same to the member on Gyges who complained that his voyeur suit had gone wrong, and because it was stuck at the invisible setting, he couldn't read the brand name on the label— would we test all the makes on the market and tell him which kind has the switch under the left arm? But during his enforced imperceptibility he was run down by a rocket sled. *De mortuis* . . .

Having had this rather gloomy picture of the outcome of our survey painted for you, you may now be asking, "Was there any point in mounting it anyway?"

We are delighted to say that the answer is a resounding "yes!"

If it did nothing else, the survey showed us that we have been unforgivably neglectful of the true requirements of a very large proportion of our subscribers. We can only apologize for this and plead that one of the lessons we hoped to derive from the survey was to discover the nature of our median member.

Obviously, our *average* subscriber would be a nonsensical compound creature—to be exact, one and two-thirds of a married female with an annual income of 2,800 credits, a batch of hoopoe eggs and seven-eighths of a hectare of reed matting, chiefly interested in the Zagnabovian question, potlatch, and the superior merits of strychnine over prussic acid as a seasoning for beef Bourguignon.

Our statisticians did, however, advise us that we could hope to determine a typical person who corresponded to the largest possible number of the membership. Somewhat to our surprise, when we punched the computer for this information, we discovered that our median is a citizen of Luxor, Lonestar or Eldorado, with an income of 27,000,000 credits, taking the deluxe calf-bound vellum edition of this journal with hand-tooled gilt lettering on the spine and built-in pentasensory commentator—in quintuplicate or sextuplicate so that there would be a copy of each month's issue for every member of the family, often including the dog! Very nearly one in three of the entire membership, reported the computer, fits this general description.

Frankly, we were astounded. The level of affluence on those planets is so high that palladium-plated spaceboats are marketed by Neiman-Marcus-Harrods-Wojcecenski not in pairs but in groups of three labeled "His," "Hers" and "Its", so that the odd one can be thrown in the garbage on delivery.

Why, we asked ourselves, should *Good Buy*—dedicated to helping people secure maximum return for minimum outlay—be so popular on worlds where it doesn't make any difference at all whether what people buy is fit for use or not? (Except insofar as there is a risk of overloading garbage-clearance facilities—but even that doesn't seem especially significant. Most people there own robotic disposers that automatically shunt refuse into the local sun.)

And then we received a note, along with a copy of our questionnaire, picked out in individual diamonds on inch-thick lead plates and expressed to us by Class Triple A* galactic mail (which costs three thousand credits per gram), from which we discovered the explanation.

We have had to edit the letter slightly, but the gist of it was as follows.

Why the [deleted] don't you [deleted] Earthside [deleted] get your heads out of that heap of [deleted] and catch on to what [deleted] like us really want? If my three-year-old daughter hadn't started to try and eat her copy of your last issue, it would have gone straight in the chute as it usually does and I wouldn't have seen your questionnaire!

I don't want to be told how to economize! I subscribe to your publication purely because I can always do with having expensive things shipped to me from distant worlds like Earth. (By the way, do you know where I could order a live blue whale not less than twenty meters long? Or a pair of Indian elephants would do, in a pinch?)

Sorry. I'm being too hard on you. At least you take the trouble to quote nice exorbitant terms.

Look, the problem here is this. According to our tax laws, every Midsummer Day the government takes away all the money you haven't managed to spend since last time. It's a great way of minimizing bureaucratic interference with the daily lives of our citizens, not having sales taxes and income taxes and all that other [deleted]. But think what happens if we don't spend enough!

Lord, it's hard to find things one can buy as it is. If the government, armed with all the surplus revenue it collects from the citizens as I explained before, were to start bidding against private individuals, there wouldn't be anything left for us at all!

Sure, charity donations are tax deductible—in theory. But the last planetary census showed that the lowest income anyone had filed was four and a half million credits, and that wasn't even for a human being, but a canary! How the blazes do you operate a charity under those conditions?

And gifts are tax deductible, too. You find me someone who's willing to take a present from me, though! If anybody offered to give me a few million credits, I'd *run*. I don't think I'd even stop to get in a rocket, in spite of having a fleet of thirty of them. (Or possibly forty—I think I ordered some more the other day.)

I'm going out of my skull, believe me! Right now I have the builders in—they're doing over the east wing in neo-rococo. But it's the third time I've had to rebuild the house this financial year, and I kind of liked the Moorish style we had before the pseudo-brutalist installed last month. Only I couldn't afford to keep on with it! As a result, here I am with rain streaming in through the cracked marble ceiling, trying to stop my daughter from breaking her neck on the floor of the sub-basement (sixty meters deep and due to be enlarged tomorrow) while they stick up all kinds of hideous gold and red fretwork in place of the black and white bricks they're scrapping. I have to do a lot of traveling—it's a good way of getting rid of extra credits—but once in a while I'd like to recognize my home when I come back to it!

To cap the lot, I see on the morning news where the unions are threatening to strike for lower pay, and this blasted socialist government of ours always assesses tax deductions at the current union scale. If they stay on strike until the tax year ends, moreover, I can't legally pay them anything!
Help! HELP!!!

Yours faithfully [signed]:
Getty C. Midas XXXIII

In face of a heartfelt cry like that, what decent being could refrain from coming to the rescue? As an interim measure, we have quadrupled the subscription rates for the deluxe edition, and expressions of gratitude are already coming in. But we don't propose to stop there. Plans are afoot to produce an ultra-de-luxe edition on hydroscopic paper with soluble ink, guaranteed to become illegible within fifteen minutes of leaving the presses, so that indefinite repeat orders can be filed with no prospect of ever actually receiving a legible copy. And as of next month we shall start to issue a special supplement to *Good Buy*, entitled *Extravaganza*, printed in thirty-six-point type on platinum sheets, and dedicated to the ringing, clarion call of our new slogan: "The more you spend, the less you get"

Getty C. Midas, do not despair! The Consolidated Galactic Federation of Consumers' Associations is on your side!

NOBODY AXED YOU

I felt so detached and critical, it was almost as though I were watching someone else chopping open Denise's head. That was a knack I'd acquired through long experience. Detached or not, though, I felt elated. This was good! This was the most wonderful thing I'd ever done!

I could feel the hot, sweat-slippery handle of the hatchet threatening to slip from my grasp as I swung it again and again. I could feel the slimy stickiness of blood on my hands. It sprayed all over my shirt and jacket and made the synfab stick to my chest. I could smell its sickly scent.

Fabulous!

She was dead, there could be no doubt. Probably the first swing of the hatchet would have been enough. But I had to make sure. Then the next step would be to dismember her and put her in the disposal tube before anyone came in—

"Gardner! Where the hell are you? Gardner! Say, have you seen Gene Gardner anywhere?"

I sighed and switched off the runback machine. The picture hesitated and froze at a frame showing me bending over Denise's body prior to taking off the legs. I remembered that was where I'd hesitated when actually recording the scene, because the lab had done a magnificent job with the dummy and those legs were so exactly like Denise's that I'd had a momentary qualm. But it hadn't spoiled the total effect.

I put the lights up and got out of my seat—the middle one in the row. Blast Bossman Crane for interrupting! But when he shouted in that voice, making the whole building shake, it wasn't good to make him wait around.

I slid the door back in its grooves. There he was on the stairs, puffing and panting and glowering, his mock cigar jutting up at a warning angle. Behind him his two secretaries (as an affectation, he had identical twins, both blonde, both beautiful) hovered with recorders at the ready, while all about him the leisure-time shifters huddled against the wall and the balusters, trying to give him more room than there was.

"Looking for me, Mr. Crane?" I called.

"Might have guessed!" he barked. "Damn narcissist!" He came charging up the steps, thrust past me into the runback room, and stopped as though a brake had been applied by remote control.

"And on your own, too!" he grunted. "On your own!" His tone was indictment and sentence combined.

"The hell!" I said, nettled. I pointed to a shrouded heap on the floor behind the seats.

"What's that?" Crane demanded. The heap moved irregularly, then seemed to become aware of the situation and froze.

"Couple of leisure-time shifters got married today," I explained. "Asked could they honeymoon in here under that cover. I said why not, provided they kept decently quiet."

"Well, the honeymoon's over," Crane snapped. "I want a talk with you in private. Get 'em out of here," he added to the nearer of his secretaries.

She exchanged a glance with her sister, and they both blushed. As a matter of principle, of course, Crane's personal staff and most of the front people of the organization at least pretended to be frigid; in the girls' case, it wasn't pretense. On the fiery red of their cheeks the F symbols stood out vividly.

"Ah, hell!" Crane said, realizing. He gave the honeymoon couple a prod with his toe. "Back to the stairs, you! And thank Mr. Gardner for letting you in here, why don't you?"

Sheepishly they emerged from under the cover, fastening zips and so on. The girl was rather pretty, I thought. I couldn't call her beautiful and mean it, though. Denise was so staggeringly lovely, I was getting into the habit of reserving that category just for her.

The couple muttered obedient thanks and left. A ribald chorus of congratulations welled up outside before one of the secretaries could get to the door and slam it.

"Why in hell don't you make things more difficult for 'em, instead of easier?" Crane sighed. "Ah, well—we all have our lapses, and a weakness for romance isn't cured in a day."

He dropped into the middle seat facing the screen, the good one where I'd been sitting, and jabbed his mock cigar toward the frozen picture.

"If I didn't know you better, Gene," he said, "I *could* hope you were running through that stinker to find out what was wrong with it. But I guess you were basking in your own brilliance, as usual."

I stared at him. It wasn't a joke—Crane had a special ponderous tone for jokes, like an elephant dancing.

"Stinker?" I echoed. "Now, look here, Bossman—"

"Have you heard the DOA rating on that show yet?" he cut in.

I hesitated. I hadn't, in fact; I had no reason to think it had fallen below standard, though. Did Crane's outburst mean there had been some catastrophic drop in the DOA's? I hadn't answered before he drew his mouth up in a sneer.

"Not worried about the figures any more, hey? Play back the rating for him, you two!"

The girls, their faces pale and calm as usual, the F symbols barely discernible on their pinky skin, took station about five feet apart on either side of the screen—for stereo, of course—and at a nod from Crane switched their recorders on. The voice of Jud Logan, the DOA rating expert, rang out.

"This week the Gene Gardner *Show-to-Kill-Time* rated eight hundred sixty dead on arrival within forty-eight hours of airing. Weekly average since this time a year back: seven hundred twenty-one decimal four. This week's subject: axe murder."

The recorders clicked off. Relieved but still puzzled, I rounded on Crane. "What's wrong with that?" I demanded. "It's up on last week, it's over the year's average —it always is! Show me anyone who gets a better DOA every week on the week!"

He wasn't in a reasonable mood. He clamped the mock cigar back in his mouth. "You know how much the population of the city area went up in those same twelve months? Four hundred and eighty thousand! Have you been out and about recently? Have you *tried* to get about? Or have you been sitting admiring yourself in runback?"

"Admiring myself! That be damned, Bossman! You want I should take myself to Lancaster, maybe? His top DOA rating for any network show is ninety or a hundred below mine. Who dreams up these shows? Who keeps them ahead of the field week in, week out? I do! Doing better than anyone else in the business—that makes it a crime not to cure the problem single-handed?"

He wilted. I was glad. I had a recurrent nightmare in which he actually told me to go back to Harold Lancaster at our biggest rival network. He was still a better boss than Lancaster had ever been to me when I was serving my apprenticeship, before I rated star billing, let alone my own show. So, to keep him sweet, I dropped the pressure.

"Okay, points made on both sides. Of course, the show isn't perfect. I hope it never will be, because improving it is what gives me the zest to keep it rolling forty-eight weeks in the year. But I'm always willing to listen to outside ideas, you know. Why don't you and I and the girls sit down and watch this one you called a stinker, clear through from the start, and see if we can brainstorm a few new slants?"

He sighed. "I've seen it four times already. But I guess I can stand another dose. Come where you can see, you two," he added to the secretaries.

I triggered the chair-arm switch and ran the recording back to the main title at the beginning.

"I'll keep the sound down," I said, "and I'll stop it occasionally to explain the thinking behind a particular episode, right? Now, is there anything you don't like about the main title? You see we have my name in white and the initial 'S' of the title itself, and then the word 'Time'; everything else is in blood-red so it stands out—*SHOW-TO-KILL-TIME*."

One of the girls ventured, "Couldn't you hold the red lettering by itself after the white has faded, so there's no room for mistake?"

"It's an idea," I agreed. "I'll ask the psychologist on the script team. He may say that having 'HOW TO

KILL' on the screen by itself is overdoing it—but I'm always open to well-meant suggestions. After all, who has a bigger interest in the show's success than I have?"

The girls chuckled in unison. If it hadn't been for Denise, I'd have been very interested to find out how accurate their F symbols were.

I went on commentating on the show, explaining how the dialogue was checked with word- and phrase-frequency lists published by a reliable research outfit, so I could be absolutely sure the same dialogue, word for word, might occur in daily life; how the settings were checked for authenticity by social workers; how the weapon selected —as always in these shows—was a common one, readily purchasable; how the killer, myself, was shown marking himself beyond doubt as he did the job, so that anyone could see him and turn him in to the law, thus insuring that not only the victim but also the killer contributed to diminishing the total population.

Despite saying this one was a stinker, Crane couldn't fault it on a single point. I felt more flattered by his silence than by any DOA rating I'd ever picked up.

Toward the end I stopped the picture where it had been when Crane interrupted me. "You'll notice what a good job the props lab does on our dummies," I said. "Even the internal organs are exact—they have to be, naturally, because in many of the shows they're exposed to the cameras. I'm very proud that making these dummies gives full employment to no less than sixty people."

Crane and both girls nodded approval. Neither they nor I had to worry about adequate work, but it was impossible to avoid a stir of sympathy for those who did.

"Mr. Gardner," said the girl who hadn't made the suggestion about the titles, "we notice you always use Miss Denise Delarose in your shows, and she's generally the victim. Wouldn't it be a good idea to change the victim sometimes?"

I gave her a sharp look. The suggestion wasn't a serious one, for sure; I put it down to wanting to say something after her sister had done so, and to plain ordinary jealousy. Put these two, attractive as they were, in the same room with Denise, and they practically disappeared from sight.

"We do 'change the victim,'" I pointed out curtly. "In one show out of every four there's a multiple killing, and also in one show out of four the victim is a man. I've even played the victim's role myself on occasion, though not for some months because it had a poor effect on the DOA rating. People apparently couldn't take the killing seriously if they saw the star of the show die. Besides, there's a psychological reason for making the victim a beautiful woman. The more attractive she is, the more likely she is to—uh—" I saw them begin to blush and fidget, sighed, and settled on the polite circumlocution. "The more likely she is to increase the population," I said. "So we stress pretty women as potential victims."

I glanced at Crane, and my heart sank. He really was in a hole-picking mood! He was going to take what the girl had said as though it were a sensible comment.

"How many times has Denise played the victim in the past few months?" he rapped.

I couldn't hedge on that. "Twelve times in the past six months, not counting multiple killings which included her."

"Harrumph! If people can't take the killing seriously when the star gets killed, how can they take it seriously when the same victim crops up all the time?"

"Well, for one thing, Denise is a magnificent actress! And we take pains to ensure that every role is as different as can be from the one before it."

"Fair enough. But how different from the role before *that*, Gene?"

I was sweating now. "Well, we can't have *too* great a diversity, you know. We're always aiming at a maximal number of potential identifications, so we have to select roles from the high-density social strata and the most overpopulated classification groups."

Crane grunted. "I've heard all that before," he said obstinately. "The point's still valid. Suppose you—"

I saw I was going to have to dig my heels in.

"No supposing!" I said bluntly. "The show wouldn't have got where it is if we'd 'supposed' and fired blind. I say stick to facts. And facts are that the rating is higher these past six months, since Denise has been playing opposite me, than it's ever been before. Facts are that Denise and I inspire one another—working with her, I really live the part. Look!"

I gestured at the screen and tripped the switch on the seat arm. "Did you notice that check in my movements? A pang of remorse! A moment of hesitation as the killer realizes what he's done! Is that or is it not true to life?"

Glancing at the girl who had started the argument, I saw she wasn't willing to be convinced. Some people— mostly attractive women—don't believe attractive women can act. Denise was an exception. I set out to ram the fact home.

After a quarter-hour's hard selling, I'd tried every angle of attack I could think of, and I hadn't made out. Well, I'd just have to figure out more to use tomorrow.

Of course, I *could* always go back to Lancaster and take the show with me . . . If it meant keeping Denise, I could force myself to do it.

One of the girls interrupted discreetly to remind Crane of an appointment due in a few minutes. Shrugging, he got up.

"Leave it as is for the moment, Gene," he said. "Believe me, I'm not quarreling with your ability or your rating. I'm just looking for ways to jack that rating up still further—past the thousand, maybe!"

Yes, it would be quite something to have the first show to hit the magic number. I gave a wan smile.

"I appreciate that, Bossman. Still, we've come a long way already from our first rating—remember?"

He remembered, all right. Forty-two! In fact, after that first show there was talk about canceling the series immediately. But Crane had faith in me, and I had to admit I owed him a lot for that. The first show was a poisoning, and the choice of that method was a mistake. The second was a straightforward stabbing with a butcher knife, and within forty-eight hours the rating was a hundred percent up on the first week: eighty-five butcher-knife victims DOA in the city area. And the third week we topped the hundred, and never looked back.

But I still swore it had taken Denise's arrival in the show to put it right ahead of the competition.

On the point of leaving, Crane paused and turned. "Gene!" he called. "What's the theme for the next show?"

Spreading my hands, I grinned. "I'll sweat it out by first rehearsal tomorrow," I said. "You know how I work."

"I'd like it ahead of time," he said. "I have a policy conference tomorrow at ten. The sponsors' group want to put your show on the agenda. I don't know why, and I was going to object, but instead of that, let's have you sitting in on the discussion, okay?"

All I could do was look delighted.

Only a few of the things which I'd got out of the success of the show meant anything to me in themselves—except getting Denise, which meant everything. The car was one of the few. I really appreciated not having to fight for subway places or room on a bus any more. Although I'd had it nearly a year now, I still had to stop and admire it for a moment every time before I got in. Long—at least ten feet—roomy, with plenty of space for four adults, it was barely smaller than the Bossman's own, and one of only a few thousand similar models in the city. Of course, it was attention-getting, and that had its drawbacks.

Like this evening. I collected my regular passengers from the transport coordination depot—two young men who worked in the public-relations section and lived a short distance beyond my home—drove out of the building and hooked on to the end of a chain going to the intersection of Plane and Fifteenth.

"Picking up Denise!" I explained to the passengers. They didn't raise any objection—the detour would only take an hour or so, and after all it was my car, not theirs.

At first we got along quite quickly, the speedo hitting as high as twelve m.p.h. Then at the usual jam around Plane and Tenth we slowed to a crawl. On the packed sidewalk someone noticed that the seat beside me was empty. He came over and rapped on the window. Of course, I couldn't hear what he said, the car being soundproof, but other people could—other loafers idling around on the sidewalk. Within a few seconds a fair crowd had gathered: nine hundred to a thousand, I judged.

I could tell from their contorted faces that they were being worked up to a fever pitch by the man who had started the trouble. I glanced in the rearview mirror and saw that my passengers' lips were moving nervously.

There was no real call to worry, I was sure. Once the crowd began to interfere with traffic, the police would show in seconds. Which they did. A few bursts from an automatic weapon put the pedestrians back where they belonged, apart from about half a dozen who got trampled in the rush, and the original troublemaker, who stood his ground obstinately, yelling at the police and pointing at me.

I rolled down the window as an officer approached. He recognized me, naturally, and as soon as I'd explained that the seat was empty because I was picking up Denise, he apologized, shot the troublemaker, and got back aboard his 'copter.

So in spite of the fuss I was only a few minutes late at my rendezvous with Denise. I had no idea where she'd been all day—shopping, perhaps; she could afford to shop occasionally now, and I wasn't going to rest till she could do it at least once a week.

If she had been shopping, she'd found a bargain, that was for sure. Her eyes were sparkling, and the way she kissed me on getting in to the car told me she was on top of the world. In fact we'd rolled a dozen blocks before I realized we ought to have hooked on somewhere else by now and turned toward home.

Laughing, I made her hold back the big news till I'd sorted the problem out, and then gave her my best camera smile.

"What's with you?" I demanded. "I haven't seen you in such a state since we got married!"

"Then that's your fault," she teased me. "And so's this, so we're even. Isn't it wonderful? The clinic says definitely yes!"

"What?" I said, and felt as though I'd suddenly gone hollow clear through.

"They say yes! And it's sixty-forty in favor of a boy. It's too early to be sure, but—"

"A what?" I said.

"A boy—a son! Gene, I'm so happy! Directly I was finished at the clinic, I went right next door to the maternity guidance room and got all their literature—look, I have it here, marvelously comprehensive—and some

books and some educational tapes. I put one straight in
the recorder, just as a treat for myself. Listen! Can't you
imagine how wonderful it's going to be hearing Gene
Junior lisp through his first nursery rhymes?"

She held up her recorder and pressed the *on* switch
before I could stop her. A silly, patronizing female voice
filled our half of the car with a graceless song:

> "What is the F on your cheek, pretty maid,
> My pretty maid, my pretty maid?
> The F stands for 'frigid,' sir, she said,
> Sir, she said, sir, she said,
> The F stands for 'fri-i-gid,' sir, she said!"

I made to switch the nonsense off, but she put the
recorder out of my reach, and remembering that the passengers in the rear seat could see us even if they couldn't hear
us, I didn't try to grab. I sat there, fuming, while the
second verse played to its end.

> "Then I can't marry you, my pretty maid,
> My pretty maid, my pretty maid.
> Nobody axed you, sir, she said,
> Sir, she said, sir, she said,
> CHOP cherry CHOP cherry CHOP! CHOP! CHOP!"

"I liked that one specially," Denise said brightly, turning off the recorder. "It reminded me of last week's show."

I took a deep breath. "Are you out of your mind?" I
said.

"Gene!"

"You must be!" In the time the tape had taken to play,
I'd had the chance to get boiling mad. Now I blew up.
"What in hell do you think it's going to do to the show's
DOA rating if it gets around that the stars are increasing
the population? Hey? Do you know what I've been doing
all afternoon? I've been fighting an attempt by Bossman
Crane to squeeze you out of your regular spot in the
show! I thought I was on the way to winning, and you
come along and tell me this and expect me to grin and
bear it! Hell, do you think you'll be able to hide the state
you'll be in a few months from now? And even if you
could, what's the point of trying if you've been stupid
enough to go to a clinic instead of finding out the name

of a reliable and discreet MD? Those places are hotbeds of gossip, and it'll take a week to kill the rumors that have started already, I'm damned certain of that—Denise!" I switched to a pleading note. "Denise, are you completely insane?"

She was staring at me frozen-faced. I recognized her unjustly-accused expression; it was in two shows out of four on a fair average.

"Gene, you're the one that's crazy—either that or so unnatural I don't believe it. A man who hears he's due to be a father is supposed to be pleased, not—"

"Supposed!" I raged. "I spent the afternoon telling Crane not to *suppose* things! Now you're doing it! Four hundred eighty thousand the population's gone up lately in this city alone—God knows what the figure is for the whole country. And here we are priding ourselves on a DOA rating that's doing something to stop the rot, and you let yourself get pregnant"' I buried my head in my hands. "Doesn't the show mean *anything* to you? Don't you care about the purpose it serves?"

"The show's fiction," she countered, but a quaver in her voice indicated I'd made a dent in her abnormal mood. I hurried to make it a crack.

"Fiction! Why, only a few minutes back a sidewalk loafer practically started a riot because that seat where you're sitting was empty and he was on foot. The police had to turn out and half a dozen people got trampled. Fiction? Fiction hell! The show exists for a purpose—it's one of the things helping to make the world a fit place again. I *believe* in that show and the good it does; if I didn't, I couldn't have built it and *you* up to the top rating it has now. It's a hell of a sight more than just fiction, hear me?"

She turned in her seat and stared through the windshield at the train of cars ahead. I'd seen this look of withdrawal before, too—on dozens of shows. That didn't stop me being hurt by it. I had a moment of mental struggle. Then I put my hand on hers, finding it curiously limp and cold.

"I'm sorry, darling," I said. "I blew my top."

She didn't give any sign that she'd heard me. I went on, "Look, if you think it over, you'll come to see I'm right.

We can get things fixed, and I'll see that the news is publicized enough to kill any rumors that got started this afternoon, and—tell you what! How long would this damned thing have taken to arrive? Nine months, isn't it?"

Her pale lips barely moved. "Eight, now," she whispered.

"It's a good long time! By then, believe it or not, at the rate we are developing we should pass the thousand mark. A thousand DOA's out of one show—isn't it wonderful? I'll milk the sponsors of a bonus for that, and we'll have the most terrific celebration, and you'll be able to forget that I ever made you unhappy. I really am sorry, darling. But you gave me a terrible shock, you know. You made me very afraid and miserable for a moment there."

I'd assumed it was just a mood. Denise got these fits of the blues sometimes, when the apartment got her down because after all it wasn't as big as it could have been, or when too many people recognized her on the street and she had to be rescued before she was mobbed. Me, I was adjusted to that—the more often I was recognized, the better for my morale.

Only . . . this was pretty long-lasting, for a blue mood. And she'd picked a hell of an evening to stage it, too. First rehearsal due tomorrow at fifteen hours, and by then I had to have the plot of the week's show cut and dried so we could script and select props and get the scenery into production ready for recording next day. I couldn't turn on my creative faculties with Denise mooning about the way she was, and I'd got to. Absolutely got to. If I didn't show with a dilly of an idea when the policy conference met at ten, I wouldn't be able to scotch this notion of replacing Denise. (Though I wasn't as fierce about this proposal as I had been earlier.)

I tried changing the subject. I tried appealing to her in so many words to come off her high horse. I tried putting suggestions for the show to her for her opinion. She just went on moping.

At twenty-one hours I gave up, dropped into my viewing chair in the middle of the apartment and tried to cajole her into sitting on my knee to watch the competition's best-rated show the way we usually did together. She wasn't having that either. She pulled a face and sat down on the divan behind me.

So the hell with it. I wasn't going to pass up the rival show to accommodate her tantrums. I switched on, just in time to catch the intro music and the titles.

Lancaster's big DOA show was quite different from mine. It relied on guest stars, which I'd always said was wrong. How could you expect the viewers to identify if they saw people on their wall-to-walls they'd seen already in scores of widely differing roles? Nonetheless, the Lancaster team sometimes came up with a good idea, and to add to my depression, tonight was one of their better nights.

The main character was a janitor living in what used to be the elevator car of a big apartment building. He was presented as a socially well-adjusted type. One of the fifty-odd people living on the twelfth floor was a pretty girl he'd fallen for. But because he was afraid he might lose control of himself if he struck up an acquaintance with her, and maybe get her in private and run the risk of increasing the already unbearable population density in the block, he'd never even spoken to her.

Then a heel living on the floor below this girl started to hang around her, and the janitor was appalled to find that she—whom he'd pictured to himself as decently frigid —was letting him make time with her. He brooded and kept watch till he was sure beyond doubt. Then, heavy-hearted, he went into action.

On the landing at the foot of the stairway between the twelfth floor, where the girl lived, and the eleventh, where the heel lived, was a man-high window coming almost to the floor, which used to give on the fire escape before it was taken away under the municipal ordinance a few years back. He freed the catch on this window and oiled the hinges so it swung easily. Then he got some grease and smeared it all over the stairs.

The gimmick, naturally, was that, when the heel came back to his own floor after being with the girl, he'd slip and go straight out the window to smash on the sidewalk eleven floors below. Ingenious. And the shots of the stairway were very atmospheric.

Then there was a good comic sequence as the janitor

waited to see his rival come out—only just about everyone else on the twelfth floor beat him to it: a gang of kids, then a fat woman with a huge ration bag (indicating a big family), then a couple of men a few moments apart. And the way the camera caught the look on the janitor's face as he patiently pulled the window to after each failure and slopped more grease on the stairs was as fine a job as I'd seen in years.

My envy began to get lost in honest professional admiration round about the fourth time an unwanted victim skidded on the stairs and went looping out the window. This was very well done, except for the music, which seemed incongruous—

The music?

I snapped around in my viewing chair. Sure enough, the music didn't belong with the show at all. Denise was playing that damned tape again, the one I'd heard in the car:

"Nobody axed you, sir, she said,
CHOP cherry CHOP cherry CHOP! CHOP! CHOP!"

"Denise!" I said politely. "I'm viewing—please turn that off."

She paid no attention. I sighed, got up and took the recorder from her limp grasp. I dropped the tape cassette in the waste disposal tube, patted her cheek and returned to my chair just in time to catch the climax. The girl and the heel emerged from the girl's room together, arms around each other, smiling, and duly lost their footing on the greasy stairs. Together they went diving through the window, the heel revealing his true nature as he tried to save himself at the girl's expense. Cut to the janitor's ludicrous expression as he realized his plan had worked too well.

So that left him to get his comeuppance. It came as he leaned out to pull the window closed; he leaned too far, overbalanced—and over a last shot of the swinging window the credits came up.

I bit my lip. The only flaw in the whole thing was that a careless viewer might have taken the janitor's demise as voluntary, and suicide was against the production code. It wasn't enough of a fault to signify. The beautifully generalized setting was bound to insure a surge of people breaking their necks on greased stairways in the next couple of days, and that meant a big boost to the Lancaster show's DOA rating.

Damn them! I'd been struggling to work out a show involving a janitor for months, and the best I'd been able to do called for arson, which was out of the question. If a fire broke out spontaneously, it was acceptable to take advantage of it—by not having fire escapes, for example. But living accommodation was far too scarce for me to be able to build a show around a deliberately started fire.

I turned to Denise. "Were you watching, honey?" I inquired. "You see the kind of talent we're up against, and why we dare not let anything happen that would harm the show!"

She didn't answer. She didn't say anything else all evening.

My head felt apt to crack open next morning. I was in a hell of a state when I arrived early at the studios. The way Denise was behaving had prevented me from concentrating at all, and yet somehow I had to dream up a better situation than the one Lancaster had used last night—by ten hours, when the policy conference met.

More than once when I was blocked I'd found inspiration in going through the prop labs and storerooms. Starved of any other idea, that was where I went.

I was usually on good terms with the sixty technicians in the lab who weekly turned out the dummies for the show—so incredibly lifelike they could do everything but walk and talk. But this morning, directly I came into the lab, I felt veiled hostility in the air. No: not so much hostility as a lack of the ordinary respect. Something in that man's smile, which could have been a sneer if it were more pronounced. And instead of a big smile and a cheery greeting from the girl who styled the dummies' hair, a mere nod.

I told myself I was on edge, and my feeling was illusive. It wasn't till I'd reached the stockroom and met the props chief, Al Bazeley, that I discovered it wasn't just my imagination.

On catching sight of me, his long face lit with an expression I couldn't make out. Almost, he looked relieved to see me. He didn't say why, though; his only words were, "Morning, Gene. What can we do for you this early in the day?"

"Looking for an idea, as usual," I answered. "I'd like to go through the weapons section."

He nodded and fell in beside me in silence as I ambled among the racks in the stockroom. Most of the racks here held weapons: cutlasses, rapiers, knives of every kind, guns from muskets to hunting rifles to pistols to submachine guns. There were cases with bottles of poison, surgical instruments, scissors, shears, models of agricultural implements—in short, everything deadly from cars to cyanide.

There were little labels on most of the items, in half a dozen colors. Blue indicated that we'd used them in the show already. Red, and the remaining colors, indicated that such items had been used by Lancaster and other competing networks. I was depressed to see how many Lancaster-red labels there were.

I stopped in front of a rack on which lay a sleek, deadly-looking firearm I didn't recognize.

"New acquisition, Al?" I demanded.

He came back from a preoccupied trance and lifted the gun from its rack, nodding. He handed it to me so I could feel how snugly it fitted the user's grip.

"Pretty rare weapon, that," he said with pride. "Forty-shot carbine. I heard of its existence a year ago, but I only got hold of it last week. That's the magazine alongside the stock, see? And the single-to-rapid control is here where you can touch it with your trigger finger. Notice how light and easy it snicks over? The whole thing's in impeccable condition."

It was certainly a keen weapon. "You have shells?" I asked.

"Case of a hundred twenty that came with the gun—three full loadings. Say, Gene, this is a hell of a thing to have to ask a friend, but—"

A sort of icy block formed around my heart. I knew what was coming even before I'd said heartily, "Go ahead,

Al! Ask me anything you like. You know I don't offend easily."

"Well—there's a peculiar rumor going around about Denise." He swallowed and cocked his head on one side.

"Such as?" I encouraged. *Damn* the scandalmongers at the clinic! Whatever happened to so-called medical ethics?

"People are saying she's—uh—due to add to the population. She and you, naturally."

"Oh, that!" I said scornfully. "Migawd, Al, I wish our DOA rating would grow as fast as rumors do! Like all rumors, this one's built on a grain of truth, granted—but accidents can happen to anybody."

"Accident?" echoed Al doubtfully.

"Pure accident," I emphasized. "And, of course, there are ways to fix such accidents, which we'll be doing forthwith. Neither of us is crazy enough to jeopardize the show."

Unexpectedly he put out his hand. "I sure am glad to hear you say that, Gene!" he exclaimed. "Look, in absolute confidence, I've had the same kind of trouble. My wife's been arguing with me all the past month because I want her to fix another—uh—accident. She's a tremendous admirer of yours. Would you let me tell her what you've just told me? Then I'm sure I'll be able to persuade her."

I didn't fancy letting the word get about till I'd had an okay from public relations on the phrasing of it. Still, Al was an old friend . . . I nodded permission. "I guess it's in the public interest," I said.

At ten I had to go to the policy conference, and I still hadn't had an inspiration for the week's show. I sweated all the way to the conference room, wondering about hit-and-run drivers, people starting riots in which others got trampled, and a score of themes beside—all perfectly acceptable but far too expensive. It took twelve hours to get a camera crew to and from a location outside the city and far enough distant to ensure that lens mugs didn't ruin the effect, so I was limited to two location shows per year. No, it had to be a studio job.

Oh, I was definitely in for a bad time.

Big as the room was, it was crowded, and I sat knee to

knee with Crane on his side of the table. Behind him were his two secretaries, identical smug smiles on their faces. I gave them a dirty look as I entered, for the sake of whichever of them had suggested ousting Denise.

I was sure Crane had seen the Lancaster show last night. I knew from the glower he maintained unbroken.

Across the table the expressions weren't dirty; they were just tough. On the left was the sponsors' group spokesman, Mabery of Monopoly Manufacturers Inc. Next to him was Jackson Weems, representing the government and the Commission on Communications. And at the right, stony-faced, wearing the black robes of the Order of Spiritual Sanctimony, was Brother Louis Gravamen, adviser on morality for the network. Much to my astonishment, he gave me a stony smile and a nod as I sat down. He wasn't in the habit of doing that very often.

Each of these three also had a secretary with him. As Crane cleared his throat to begin the meeting, five clicks indicated the switching on of recorders.

Crane explained why I'd been invited to sit in and asked if there were objections to my being present throughout the part of the agenda which wasn't concerned with my show. I hoped there would be, to give me another thinking space. But nobody minded, so we went ahead.

Minor problems took up the first half hour. Brother Louis had viewer complaints on moral grounds about a commercial for one of Mabery's products, and a suitable modification was agreed. Then Weems raised the problem of leisure-time shifters and broached a scheme to provide government-assisted viewing centers for people who couldn't get home owing to transport difficulties; naturally Mabery—whose company made home wall-to-walls, among all its other products—objected.

Schemes like this were always coming up, and people like Mabery were always saying it wasn't a question of improved viewing facilities, it was a matter of better transportation, and people like Weems were always taking this as an insult, and the inevitable result was deadlock. It was deadlock now. I let my mind wander until they got on to news coverage.

Then I pricked my ears up. It was just possible a topical theme might present itself.

Weems had an axe to grind on this subject, and soon he was blasting at Mabery for all he was worth. There had been a promising outbreak of virus plague a few weeks before, which I remembered hearing about.

"And what happened?" barked Weems. "The news bulletins were crammed with pictures of pitiable fever-ridden children instead of hopeful-looking census officers! As a direct result—I tell you, a *direct* result—before the casualty list had even hit ten thousand, one of your drug companies was marketing a specific. Where are we now? Back where we started. It hasn't taken a single life for more than ten days!"

Mabery looked uncomfortable. He didn't answer the attack directly, but appealed to Brother Louis.

"Isn't it a moral duty to fulfill a need when it arises? We had the drug and there was a demand for it—were we wrong to meet the demand?"

Brother Louis shrugged. "The question is the knotty one of ends and means," he said oracularly.

(Should the next show concern someone deliberately spreading an infectious disease? Out of the question: Lancaster would be able to challenge every single DOA credited to us.)

Mabery flared up—it was easy in the crowded room, for the temperature was rising to an uncomfortable level.

"Ends and means! Thunder, Brother Louis, if all you want is a means, you know as well as I do that we've had it for years!"

Unexpectedly, Weems supported him. "We could create an unstoppable disease tomorrow, for example, if it wasn't for mealy-mouthed opposition from people who are too selfish to make their own contribution to the general good."

After my row with Denise last night, I reflected, *I* certainly couldn't be accused of lack of personal involvement.

"That's not what I'm talking about," Mabery snapped. "As Brother Louis very well knows! I'm talking about steriline, which we've had for a decade, and which we aren't allowed to advertise. *That's* the means we need, and it's a hell of a sight more infallible than any of your stiff-necked, unctuous—"

Red rag to a bull. I winced and wished that someone

had objected to my staying for the whole conference. Now we could be sure of a long lecture from Brother Louis on our bounden duty to provide people to carry their appointed crosses.

We got it, pouring forth as hot as steel from a newly tapped furnace. According to Brother Louis, the use of drugs like steriline was morally no better than reducing the population with nuclear bombs. Even Mabery began to quiver after a while. I was a customer for steriline, of course, and had been since marrying Denise, and I felt strongly opposed to all that Brother Louis was saying, but if I'd been a practicing member of any order, I'd have been on my knees crying before Brother Louis finished.

He resumed his place with the air of one who has spoken fearlessly for the right, and there was an uncomfortable silence.

"I think," Crane ventured, "that we might leave this . . . uh . . . delicate topic and proceed with the agenda . . . ?"

A vigorous nod from Weems, a nod and scowl from Mabery, a lordly gesture of permission from Brother Louis. Their eyes turned simultaneously on me.

(Matter of interest: If Mabery was now making claims that steriline was infallible, then how . . . ?)

But Crane was charging ahead. "The sponsors' group has asked for a discussion of Mr. Gene Gardner's show today. Ah . . ."

"We support the request," Weems spoke up. "Although the shows of which Mr. Gardner's is an example perform a valuable public service, we're anxious to see their contribution increase in ratio with the gravity of the problem, and at present this is not the case. Since Mr. Gardner's show is the outstanding one of its kind, we feel it's a good place to begin our inquiry."

That sounded ominous. I gave Weems a sunny smile.

"Our interest is parallel," Mabery said. "We view with alarm the fact that Lancaster's top show, though still getting a lower DOA rating, is actually increasing its rating more rapidly than ours, and will probably overtake us in another few months."

The smile I gave him was much less sunny.

"We're fully aware of this problem," Crane declared

hastily. "In fact, Mr. Gardner and I spent a long time yesterday afternoon discussing that very point."

"And did you come up with any fresh ideas?" Mabery said.

"Well, we considered . . ." Crane leaned back in his chair so that one of the twin secretaries could whisper in his ear, and went on. "We considered some extra punch in the main titles, and——"

"Hah!" Mabery exclaimed. "That's no good! I was watching Lancaster's show last night and was tremendously impressed. It had everything the Gardner show used to have— freshness, originality, light relief, superb atmosphere. Frankly, it's my belief that after Gardner's meteoric rise he's now letting his curve flatten out."

"There hasn't been any sign of that!" I snapped.

"There has," Mabery contradicted. "Our surveys of viewer reaction show that there's a growing lack of identification due to the recurrent appearances——"

"I know what you're going to say," Crane cut in eagerly. Blast him for a bootlicking bastard! "The too-frequent appearances of Denise Delarose as the victim. I made this very point to Gene yesterday."

They looked at me. I was temped to say what was really in my mind—that if anyone attempted to squeeze my favorite partner from the show, I'd go to Lancaster and take the show with me. Fortunately I hesitated long enough for Brother Louis to stir and give me a look that by his standards was almost benign.

"As it happens, I too saw the Lancaster show last night," he said. "And I can't share your enthusiasm entirely. Granted, the self-control exercised by the main character was admirable, but the conclusion undermined the impact. One was left in two minds as to whether the janitor's demise might not have been voluntary, and suicide is against the code. This is a fault I've never observed in any show of Mr. Gardner's."

So that was why he'd smiled when I came in. I looked properly appreciative of his support.

"True enough," Mabery conceded. "But it's not the past I'm concerned with. I want to know the future plans for the show. I want to know how Gardner proposes to stay ahead of the Lancaster show."

Now I was really on the spot. I wouldn't dare generalize. I was going to have to be precise and optimistic and all the other things I didn't feel. I licked my lips and hesitated, and then, as though someone had tripped a switch in my brain, the inspiration came. Words lined my tongue ready to be spoken.

I hid my relief with a grin.

"Both you gentlemen," I addressed Mabery and Weems, "want to see my DOA rating rise. So do I. What's the crucial factor on which the rating depends? It's viewer-identification, obviously. Right?

"Up to now we've needed to concentrate on expanding our audience. In other words, we've insured good ratings by insuring that we had a large number of viewers. We've achieved this by making our settings and characters as typical and as average as we can. The highest density of population in a given social stratum, the most overfilled classification groups—these have been our starting points.

"Now the time is ripe to switch the emphasis. We have our assured audience, our millions of viewers who won't miss the show if they can help it. From here on, we have to emphasize the universality of our situations rather than of our characters. And we'll combine this with an appeal to the audience's aspirations.

"Let's take the show we're going to rehearse today and record tomorrow. My role is that of a socially adjusted man, more prosperous than the average, fortunate enough to have an apartment for himself and his wife, who sublimates his baser instincts by collecting firearms. You'll see this is psychologically consistent, of course. Likewise, it's got assured public appeal, combining the social virtues with the lure of luxury. How many people don't cherish a secret wish that they could indulge a hobby such as collecting guns?

"But his wife—a role which will of course be taken by Denise Delarose because it's been created with her in mind —uses all her powers of seduction to break down his self-control, and succeeds, with the appalling result that she becomes pregnant."

I glanced at Brother Louis. His eyes were gleaming. "The eternal theme!" he exclaimed. "Woman as the vessel of evil! Mr. Gardner, your inspiration amazes me."

"Is this man to suffer the rest of his life because he once yielded to temptation? That seems too harsh a fate. Yet the situation develops so that this consequence seems inevitable. At last, in unutterable despair, he does the only possible thing, and ends his wife's life before surrendering with a confession on his lips to the forces of law and order.

"And here's the angle that will put us way ahead of the Lancaster show. We're through with people just like us. We're building from now on around people who are the way we'd like to be if we were rich enough and lucky enough—and *still* we're putting them in predicaments that could happen to anyone."

"Gene, it's the greatest," Crane said with honest admiration, and I saw from the expressions on the faces across the table that I'd impressed the others too. It cost me all my willpower to stop myself wiping the sweat from my face and betraying how I felt.

When Denise came to the studios—pale, walking as if in a dream—half an hour before rehearsal time that afternoon, I broke off my discussion with Al Bazeley about the weapons collection we were going to give the killer in the show, and dashed over to throw my arms around her.

"Darling! Everything's wonderful! Thanks to you I've had the most fabulous idea for this week's show—it's going to be the start of a whole new approach, and there won't be any more talk about taking you out of the show, believe me!"

She pushed me away without force. "I wouldn't have minded," she said. "If it was going to help."

I put my arm around her waist and led her unresisting over to Al. "Silly!" I teased. "I'd have minded, and I'm sure the viewers would have minded too. Al! Show Denise the carbine we're going to use!"

Al grinned and went to fetch the gun.

"I'm even glad you had that blue mood yesterday," I enthused to Denise. "It certainly paid off. Listen, what do you think of this?"

I outlined the story. When Al brought the gun, I even began to improvise movements and dialogue, so that the idea took definite shape ahead of rehearsal time.

The one thing wrong was Denise's reaction. I'd expected her to feel the theme the way I did, on a personal level. But all she said was, "Very good, Gene. It'll be a big success."

Al drew me aside, looking worried. "Gene, is something wrong?" he whispered.

"A bit of artistic temperament is all," I bluffed. "By the time we've been through the motions, she'll catch fire like everyone else. I'm sure this one's going to be terrific all round."

Then the costumes and hairstyle people came into the rehearsal studio, and the script team with their files of word- and phrase-frequencies, and the cameramen I always used, Hank and Sammy. It was time to get down to business.

While we were discussing the shape of the story, the lab team came up as usual with the dummy and set it in a chair next to Denise so that it too could be coiffed and costumed. Much sooner than usual, things were ready for a run-through. I choked off a flow of compliments from the script team's psychologist about the choice of gun collecting as a hobby for my killer, and turned to call Denise.

And stopped, shocked beyond measure. Because for a second I genuinely could not tell which was Denise and which was the dummy in those two identical chairs.

Then of course I realized: Denise was wearing the outfit I'd seen her arrive in, and the dummy was in a studio dress. The shock passed, but it left a mark.

I'd been wrong to assume that once she got into the swing of things Denise would turn in her usual fine performance. She was so lifeless that it killed the enthusiasm I'd built up among the crew. After five abortive shots at the opening "established" scenes, I was fuming behind a calm face.

"Take five!" I shouted to the crew, and closed my hand on Denise's wrist to draw her out of sight among some sets that had been used for another rehearsal earlier in the day.

"Denise!" I hissed. "What's eating you? I might as well be playing opposite one of the lab dummies! Come to life, will you? Damn it, this theme is straight out of your own experience!"

A spark of anger showed. Good: I was breaking through.

"Then *use* a dummy!" she snapped. "What's the difference?"

"I certainly can't see any in what you've done so far today!" I retorted. "All right, let's try again—and this time, for pity's sake, try and show you mean it!"

It went a little better from then on. We worked out as far as the point where the idea of seduction crossed the wife's mind. I was going to have my back to her, studying the forty-shot carbine, which was the pride and joy of my firearms collection. Suddenly I heard her humming a tune —the same damned tune!

"Nobody axed you, sir, she said——"

I spun around. "Denise!" I exploded.

She met my gaze with all the innocence in the world. "But isn't that a good idea?" she said. "After all, I'm supposed to be thinking wicked thoughts about getting myself pregnant—isn't a nursery rhyme appropriate?"

"I think it's an excellent touch, Miss Delarose," called the psychologist on the script team, and his colleagues gave approving nods. I smiled at Denise.

"Good to see you back in form!" I exclaimed.

The full rehearsal next morning was done under the cameras exactly as the final recording would be done in the afternoon. Denise seemed quite her usual self. I joked with her, pointing to the dummy in its chair at the side of the studio, and told her about my shock of the previous afternoon.

A teasing smile came to her beautiful lips. "If you're my husband and you can't tell me from a dummy, who else could?" she demanded.

"I can certainly tell you apart in private," I answered, and tried to kiss her.

She held me off. "You're supposed to be playing a socially responsible person, remember?"

I grinned and gave in.

We usually shot these shows with two cameras, one trucking and one on a blimp. There was a master screen over the goldfish bowl that showed whatever was on camera at the moment. Hank was with the blimp as usual.

I took every chance I got when I was out of shot to glance at the master screen and imagine how it would look. It was promising. Denise seemed to have lost her bad mood completely, and by the time we were up to the point of the actual killing, she was heart and soul into her part. Some of the looks of hatred she shot at me were so violent, they almost made me stumble in my lines.

By recording time the show was close to perfection. The dummy waited in its chair, with the lab team making adjustments all the time so when the climax arrived and I shot Denise down with the carbine, nobody could possibly tell there had been a switch. We finalized the sequence of shots with Hank and Sammy, and broke for lunch.

All through the meal I kept congratulating Denise over and over, for giving me the idea, for recovering from her depression, for turning in such a natural performance. She listened absently; I took it she was preoccupied with thoughts about the show.

When we came back from the canteen, Al Bazeley was waiting in the stulio. With him was a small woman, rather plain, with a round face and a nervous manner, whom I hadn't seen around here before.

"Can I have a word with you, Gene?" Al said, coming up. I nodded and drew aside from Denise, who didn't seem to notice.

"Look, Gene," Al went on, "you remember what I said about my wife? Well, she wasn't having any. She thought I was making it up. So I . . . uh . . . arranged for her to come down and meet you and Denise and get it straight from you. I hope you don't mind."

I thought it was a bit high-handed not to have asked me before bringing his wife along. Still, I couldn't very well refuse. I said brightly, "Sure! Let me explain to Denise first, though, and make sure she has no objections."

"You're a pal, Gene," he said, looking relieved.

I caught up with Denise. She was standing before the

dummy's chair, studying her duplicate with great con-centration. I put Al's problem to her. Her face lit up.

"I'd be delighted!" she said in the warmest tone I'd heard from her all day.

"Are you certain? It's none of my doing, I promise you—the rumors must have got to Al from the clinic, and since by sheer coincidence he has the same trouble, he asked——"

"It's perfectly clear," she answered impatiently. "Is that his wife standing next to him?"

"Gene!" Al called out. "Look who's coming into the goldfish bowl!"

I looked. There was Crane, and he was no surprise—he often came to rehearsals or recordings. But with him were Brother Louis Gravamen, Jackson Weems, and Mabery.

"Hell!" I said under my breath, at the same time putting on a welcoming smile. I'd hoped to . . . well, supervise the talk between Denise and Mrs. Bazeley. No chance now.

I went into the goldfish bowl and shook hands all around. Crane explained, "We were all so interested in your new plans for the show, we decided we'd like to attend the actual performance, as it were."

"I'm flattered," I said with all the enthusiasm I could muster. I gave them a quick rundown on what they could see on the studio floor, but that wasn't what they were after. At length Mabery cleared his throat.

"I hear you insist on realism in your shows, isn't that so? I mean, you use an actual knife, or an actual gun, not studio dummies."

"That's correct," I agreed. "You might not think the viewer could tell the difference, but it creates a different atmosphere and gets me deeper into my role."

"I'd be extremely interested to see the weapon you're using this week," Mabery pursued.

Crane butted in before I could stop him. "Our props man is out there on the floor talking to Miss Delarose. I'll have him fetch the gun for you."

Which he did. Al and I had to show all the fine points of the weapon to these greedy sensation-seekers. It was at least ten minutes before I could decently remark that we were holding up the show. I'd been keeping my eye on Denise and Mrs. Bazeley; they were deep in conversation, but the goldfish bowl was soundproof and no mikes were live, so I could only guess what they were saying. At one point I saw Denise point to the dummy waiting in its chair, and Mrs. Bazeley glanced from her to it and threw her hands up in amazement.

I hoped very hard that Denise was telling the other woman what Al wanted her to hear.

It seemed things had gone all right in the end, for when Mrs. Bazeley parted from Denise I saw a calm resolute expression on her round, nervous face. Maybe she was resigned to doing the sensible thing, as Denise appeared to be.

She played the whole opening section of the show with real conviction and intensity. The only retake that was necessary was my fault—I fumbled while handling a gun from the collection Al had set up for me on the wall of the set. Even that irritating nursery rhyme which had set my nerves on edge at rehearsal seemed to fit into the pattern of the story exactly as Denise had suggested.

Inexorably events followed one another: the wife's decision to break down her husband's self-control, the seduction, the consequences, the husband's horror and despair, the wife's refusal to see reason, her glorying in what she had done. Mentally I tensed as we approached the climax: the moment when we froze, cut the cameras, and had the dummy exchanged for Denise.

As usual, Al watched from the side of the floor rather than from the goldfish bowl. His wife sat meekly next to him. Once or twice I glanced at her for a reaction—after all, she was as close to an average viewer as I'd ever had present at a recording—and I was satisfied to read the emotion in her face.

Climax! I picked up the carbine, as though driven by intolerable compulsion, and turned slowly to Denise, who saw my purpose in my eyes and fell back into a chair, her mouth opening in a wordless scream. As usual, Hank's camera was covering this crucial shot, because he had a fantastic visual memory and would remain glued to his viewfinder until the dummy had been posed so exactly no one could tell there had been a switch at all.

"Cut!" I said, relaxing. At once the lab crew picked up the dummy; Denise got slowly out of her chair, and I went to grin at Crane in the goldfish bowl and received nods of approval from the VIP guests. I always moved around instead of trying to hold the pose while the dummy was set up—I found it easy to resume an interrupted movement.

I'd had a lot of experience, of course.

Suddenly there was a shrill scream of horror, and everyone, including me, whirled to look for the source. Mrs. Bazeley was flinging up her arms and yelling, and in a moment had collapsed to the floor.

People dashed to see what the matter was. I took charge and made them stand back. Al went on his knees at her side, calling her name: "Veronica! Veronica!"

Then, of course, Crane and his companions had to add to the crowd, and things were completely out of hand for a full three minutes. In the end I had a couple of the script team carry her out of the studio to a restroom along the corridor. Al went with them. A few moments later, however, he was back, looking relieved .

"She'll be okay," he said. "I'm terribly sorry. She says she was so startled at seeing how much the dummy looked like Denise that she was frightened."

I was going to give him a piece of my mind when there came an acid growl from Hank. "If you don't calm down and get back to business Gene will forget his pose!"

"The hell you say!" I answered good-humoredly. "But you're quite right. Quiet, everyone—back to the job!"

The studio settled back to normal. Hank made ready to continue the recording. I picked up my gun and fell back into my pose, and Crane herded the visitors back in the goldfish bowl.

Just before signaling Hank to proceed, I glanced at Denise sitting in the chair the dummy had been in before. I felt a qualm. It was small wonder, really, that Mrs. Bazeley had managed to scare herself. The lab had made a fantastic job of the resemblance, especially since Denise was watching me with unblinking concentration.

From the way my sample "average viewer" had reacted, this show was sure of a good rating.

I had just finished raising the gun to firing position. I went through the build-up movement again, heard Hank click the camera switch. I froze my face into a mask of demon-driven resolve, sighted on the dummy's breast over its heart. You could have heard a pin drop. A firing-pin, maybe.

My view full of the staring, open-eyed, open-mouthed face, I squeezed the trigger.

The explosion was incredibly loud. Even though I'd fired the gun during rehearsal and discovered it was as recoilless as the makers claimed, I felt jolted. A nine-millimeter hole appeared in the dummy. Blood began to ooze around it.

Slowly, as though realizing too late what I'd actually done, I lowered the carbine and began to shake.

And the dummy smiled.

It was a triumphant smile, close to a leer. It lasted only a few seconds. Then the eyelids drifted down over the magnificent eyes as they dulled.

In death.

I didn't go on with the rehearsed movements. I turned and looked at the dummy sitting in the chair at the side of the floor. I looked back at Denise, whom I had just shot dead.

I thought of a great many things in a short space of time: how Denise had talked with Veronica Bazeley; how then Veronica had staged her faint at exactly the moment when Denise could have brought the dummy back from its new pose and resumed her own. Denise could resume poses as well as I could.

I thought of the realism I was so proud of: If I fired a gun in the show, I fired a gun. A real corpse was only logical. Fair enough, fair enough.

But if Hank hadn't been distracted like everyone else by the mock fainting woman, he'd have seen Denise changing places with the dummy. He should have stuck to his job. I raised the gun and shot Hank neatly through the neck. He gave a strangled cry of amazement and fell forward, dragging his camera around so that the master screen swam with crazy panned images.

"Gene!" Al Bazeley shouted. "Gene!"

Steriline was supposed to be infallible. That meant that Denise must deliberately have stopped taking it. By implication, Al's wife would have done the same. And he let her come to the studio, today of all days. Poor Al. I shot him about where I had shot Denise—near the heart.

Behind the window of the goldfish bowl I could see Crane and the VIPs and the technicians, petrified with terror and disbelief. I could also see them above themselves. In dying, Hank had swiveled his camera around until it was focused on them.

Al had been perfectly right. The single-to-rapid control could be adjusted by a mere touch. Next time I squeezed the trigger, the carbine sowed a line of holes all across the window of the goldfish bowl. Watching in the master screen, I saw Crane shot in the face; Brother Louis Gravamen, who was taller, in the throat; Mabery, shorter, in the face again, and Weems—who was trying to get out the door—in the back of the head. A second burst disposed of the technicians. Of course, Al had put the full forty shots into the magazine. Realism.

Then I shot Sammy, the other cameraman, as he tried to hide in a corner, and went to turn Hank's camera off before going in search of Veronica Bazeley.

The show topped the thousand that week for the first time.